BOOK of BOONCE

SON OF THE GAME

-VOLUME ONE-

ISBN 979-8-35094-507-2 eBook 979-8-35094-508-9

Foreword

I'm sitting here just thinking about when I was a kid growing up. Man I had so many to look up to. Big Dirty was always my guy. As a young guy seeing how y'all was doing it, gave the block a sense of security. I could walk to Madison Square Church and pass by some of my childhood heroes. Raw Dawg, Boonce, Big Dirty, Bing, Blue and the old head Shang.

I remember in 1997 I went to prison, and I was at Riverside, I ran into Shang. When he heard I was in quarantine, he brought me so much, and showed me so much love. Raw Dawg was at Earnest C. Brooks Correctional Facility in 1997. My first day in the penitentiary, I looked up and saw Raw Dawg. He was dropping game on me from day one. Most of the time a young guy didn't have anyone to look up to. I was fortunate to have another branch of family in my presence, giving me the rules to stay out of trouble and make it back home. I was seventeen, I'll never forget the love this family showed me. I love y'all, no doubt, can't ever do it like that again. Looking forward to getting the Book! ~Big Cheese

Acknowledgement

First and foremost, praises and thanks to God almighty, for His protection, guidance and showers of blessings throughout my life.

I would like to express my deep and sincere gratitude to my mother, father, aunts, uncles, and cousins for providing me with invaluable game. All of them have contributed to the making of this man. It was a great privilege and honor to have grown up under such tutelage. I am extremely grateful for the game they have instilled in me, and I just thank them for being there.

I am sending a heartfelt thanks to my wife for her unconditional love, friendship, and patience over the years. I would also like to thank my children and nephew for being my fountain of youth, they have become my closest friends.

My special thanks goes to my grandmother. I am extremely grateful for her love, prayers, caring and sacrifices for educating and preparing me for my future. She taught me how to feed my spirit. Her encouragement when time got rough is appreciated, and has been noted in the tablet of my heart.

Introduction

Growing up in Grand Rapids, Michigan Boonce was surrounded by The Game. A kid who came of age on the Southeast side of Grand Rapids, MI during its darkest years of drugs, violence, and abandonment, and how he navigated that traumatizing landscape to a different life.

Boonce was born into a family with a notorious reputation in Grand Rapids, MI from the west end of Oakdale St. His father and uncles were well-known figures in the city and was later sentenced to lengthy prison terms.

From infancy his life is influenced by the game, and by the time he starts high school, he makes a life-shaping choice. Soon, Boonce and the second generation of the family rise up to dominate the streets. As his day-to-day life becomes more and more anxious-he is shot and watches as family fall to prison, addiction and even death.

His identity splits in two: a hustler roaming through books, whose rep of earning money rings in the streets. He gravitates toward earlier teachings that gives him both a voice to tell the story of his young life and the knowledge he needed to create a new one. Despite the challenges he has faced, he used his OGs tutelage and his personal experience as tools to carve out his own path while reviving the legacy of his family. The challenges never stopped-but neither did Boonce.

The story you're about to read is loosely based on truth. Some of the names, characters, businesses, and events have been fictionalized for dramatic purposes. But a lot of this shit may have actually happened.

The Book of Boonce – Son of the Game

70's

It was the month of May, the year 1973, at Butterworth hos-pital in Grand Rapids, MI. A woman had been wrestling with labor pains for hours before delivering her first baby. The doctor announced,

"It's a boy!"

The game gave birth to a new healthy baby boy, and there was a fascinating life story waiting for him outside the hospital. The baby's biological parents were known in the streets as "Dean the Queen" and "Bubble Gum Red".

Dean was one of the prettiest women in Grand Rapids, MI with plenty of game, and knew how to maneuver. Her game IQ was second to none. You can easily say that the fictional character Cookie Lyon was based on the life of Dean. From her fashion sense, raw nerve, and straight shooting tell-it-like-it is style. There was no mask, she was very complicated and complex. She would stop at nothing to get what she wanted, Dean was the truth.

A couple of her brothers, "Shang" and "H", controlled the drug game in the city back in the 70's. If anybody was trying to do any business, it had to go through them. If you were from out of town you were forbidden to do business in Grand Rapids in the 70's. If an out-of-towner decided to come to the city, and tried to set up shop, they were dealt with accordingly. They would send a firm warning, by raiding the shop, and confiscating any product or weapons the outsiders were in possession of. Using strongarm tactics to apply pressure to those in charge of the operation. Their intentions were to send a clear message to whoever was contem plating on invading their market. Her brothers and their organization ruled the city with an iron fist.

Red was a clean well-dressed high yellow man with the gift to gab. He was a smooth character, a gentleman of leisure and an international player. He became close friends with Dean's brothers and were in business with them. A family-like bond had been built, he was considered a brother in their eyes. With Shang and "H" as his partners, Dean as his queen along with his clever and crafty skills, it equipped him with all the important pieces needed on the chessboard.

Red had an older blood brother who was known in the streets as "Chewing Gum Red", and he was a monster in the streets and a well-connected man. He was also a gentleman of leisure and an international player doing a lot of business out of Cleveland, OH. Before I was born, he played a major role in the Alaska Fur Company heist in Grand Rapids, MI. He and his associates made a getaway with three barracks bags or laundry bags stuffed with cash. They were eventually apprehended by a Trooper of the Ohio State Highway Patrol on the Ohio Turnpike. A registration for a black Cadillac Brougham involved in the Grand Rapids fur heist was found in their possession. FBI Special Agents presented a group of photographs to two of the victims of the robbery, Chewing Gum's photograph was one of the photos that were picked out of the group. He was convicted of armed robbery and sentenced to ten to twenty years. The streets used "Chewing Gum" and "Bubble Gum" to distinguish the two Reds when speaking of them. Some people referred to them as "Big Red" and "Little Red".

On the verge of closing out their teenage years, life was going up for Dean and Red. The fast life provided them with a luxurious way of living. They had access to an excessive amount of cash, extravagant cars, expensive clothes and everything else that came with the lifestyle. The sky was the limit, it was a picture perfect scenario. They eventually bought a new home on the southeast end of the city that was plush with luxury items and decorated with red décor.

There was a lot taking place in that house. There were after hour parties with big time gambling being held on a regular basis. Well-dressed gentlemen in suits, suspenders and shoulder gun holsters surrounded a tall, large table located in the den of the house. The dice game was like the Super Bowl with women surrounding the men as spectators. Large sums of cash were on the table, the floor, and in the hands of the participants. You heard a loud celebration from some of the men as well as disappointment from others participating with side bets. People would be dancing together, others were sectioned off in different groups while trying to talk over the music and each other. There were dinners being sold from the kitchen, and a man was always on post at the front door. Most of the parties would carry over into the early mornings. After some of those parties, I can remember my father beating the shit out of my mother. One time he was beating her ass so bad that I yelled,

"Get off my momma muthafucka!"

He immediately stopped and came over to me and knelt. As he was kneeling tears were coming down his face. He grabbed and hugged me and repeated sorry I don't know how many times. I forgave him, but I was extremely upset with him at that moment. It was the last time I witnessed him putting hands on her. Not to say that he never did it again, he just never did it in front of me. I don't think either one of them knew that I was never comfortable with them being in the same room together. To me, it seemed things were better for them both when they were apart. It had become a very toxic situation. That lifestyle tends to wreak havoc on intimate relationships.

In the meantime, and in between time, my father and uncles were moving more dog food than PetSmart. There was a whole lot of pimping going on too. They were well organized, generating massive amounts of revenue. A laundering system was established to transfer the revenue into legitimate businesses. They owned a business district, an entire block of buildings which were legitimate businesses being used as a front. They had security surveillance systems installed on all their establishments. These were not your average nickel and dime hustlers. The stakes were high in their attempt to establish an empire that would withstand the test of time. It was like your favorite television drama that you watch today, except this was real life.

I was young, but I see it so vividly. It was one time we were coming back to the house from somewhere, and when we got there, my cousin and I raced to the bathroom. When we made it to the door, it was partially open but hard to push. When we finally got it open, my godfather was lying on the floor with his foot resting against the door. He had OD'd on some of that dog food. I remember seeing the needle stuck in his arm and his head being held up by the bathtub. He laid there motionless, wearing a pair of dark brown slacks and a silk copper colored wife beater t-shirt. We ran downstairs to tell my mother and father that he was upstairs dead. They both rushed upstairs, and we followed behind them, but they told us both to go back downstairs. We stood at the bottom of the stairs watching them carry him down the stairs. My mother lost hold of him and dropped him at the bottom of the stairs. As she tussled to recover her grip, they finally managed to get him into the car and my father floored it, the tires squealed as the car pulled off. Later, that night I learned that my godfather didn't die, and was very much alive. They all said that I saved his life and treated me like a boss. To this very day I still wear that as a badge of honor. My godfather was a real slick, well-groomed, well-dressed money getting ass man. He also had the gift to gab, and the ladies loved him. He was another gentleman of leisure and an international player, one of his favorite sayings was,

"Pimp or die."

He was a bona fide Mack.

My father, godfather and uncles had a good run, but a monkey wrench had been thrown in their well-oiled machine. There was an altercation that took place, and I don't know the full details of it, but somebody was foolish enough to make a life-threatening gesture toward one of them. My uncles didn't tolerate shit like that, so you know they didn't hesitate to get active with the gunplay. One of my uncles shot the man up in broad daylight, on one of the busiest intersections in the city. He emptied every bullet that he had in his gun in the man, and somehow the man miraculously survived the onslaught of bullets.

After the incident occurred, my uncle, my father and godfather were forced to leave town and were on the run for a while. The organization had lost three of Its main arteries, costing the business a considerable amount of cash flow. The business had to be restructured. They headed down south plus a few other spots, but eventually ended up having to face the consequences. I remember being in the courtroom during my father's trial. Somehow, I was allowed to speak with him during the time of his trial, I'm not sure if it was before or after court. But as a youngster at the age of maybe like five years old, I understood the severity of the situation. It could have been the steeliness of his eyes and serious expression on my father's face that led me to that conclusion. I imagine that he never intended for me to see him in such a difficult situation.

My life changed when my father, godfather and uncle got sent off to the penitentiary. Not just my life but my mother's life changed as well. Without their presence, things had gotten difficult for her on the streets. She started slowly veering off in another direction, and eventually lost her way. I can say that she was damn sure trying, but the streets started to get the best of her. In the 70's there was a hot spot in Grand Rapids called the "Limelight". I remember going there with her and waiting there in the car for hours. A lot of the hustlers, pimps and hoes that were going in and out of the establishment knew and respected my father and uncles. They would buy me chips and all types of shit from the store that was located across the street from the "Limelight".

Some of the hoes would even come and put money directly in my hand. They would say things like,

"Ya know I gotta pay my man!"

They would look straight at me, establishing prolonged eye contact with their eyes filled with a look of admiration. As a young boy that fascinated me, made me feel special, it instilled a level of an indestructible confidence in me. I grew up believing that all women felt the same way about me. Many of the pimps and hustlers would even sit out there with me for a minute and give me some good game. People would be telling me all types of stories about their experiences with my father and uncles. Every last one of them treated me like royalty. I would witness tricks being turned left and right (men paying for sexual favors from women). That was during a time that you would see more brown codeine syrup bottles than you would see pop cans laying around.

After a while, my mother found herself in a place in life that I know for a fact that she never planned to be. It had been like a year and a half since my father and uncles went away when my mother started dating a man which resulted in my little sister being born. She was born premature. I remember seeing her for the first time in that incubator with tubes connected everywhere on her. She took my heart right then and there. After I left the hospital and made it home, I cried like a baby for my little sister. I'll never forget the day they brought her home. From that day forward, I've always felt that my little sister was my responsibility.

My mother and my sister's father had gotten lost in the sauce. The streets had just about swallowed them whole. Things started getting tough around the house for us. There were times that I was left there with my little sister by myself. It was one time that I couldn't get her to stop from crying. She wouldn't take a bottle or anything. Finally, I wrapped her up and carried her over to my grandmother's house, on Oakdale St, which was only like a half mile away, a ten- or fifteen-minute walk. This became a normal pattern for us. I had become so frustrated with the situation that I wanted the house to just disappear. My grandmother's house was my safe space and that's where I wanted to live at that time. There were other times that my mother's older sister (Big Dirty, DQ, and Red Man mother) would come to get us.

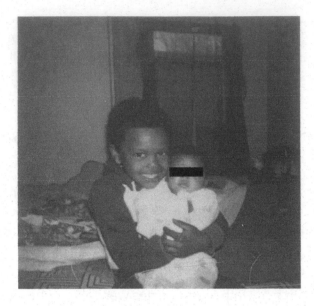

On one occasion, my mother's close friend was there visiting her, doing what they do. They summoned me to the room they were in and asked me to retrieve something from the kitchen for them. When I returned with what they requested, I noticed that there were a few books of matches lying on the table. The minute they took their eyes off me, I grabbed one of those books of matches from the table. I took the matches upstairs with me into the master bedroom, and went into the main closet, then commenced piling up clothes on the floor. I lit one of the matches then held a hair scarf over it. The scarf caught fire very quickly, then I threw it on the pile of clothes. I stood there watching as the flames slowly engulfed the pile of garments. Once the fire began devouring the clothes, I made my exit from the closet and left the house, en route to my grandmother's. The fire must have spread throughout the house rapidly, because I didn't even make it halfway there before a gentleman and my mother interrupted my escape plan. She exited the car in rage, roughed me up quite a bit before putting me in the back seat of the car. The sirens from the fire engines were screaming from every direction. To this day I get butterflies thinking about how I left my mother in the house without telling her what I had done. I never intended to bring any harm to her, I just wanted the house to disappear. I ended up moving in with my grandmother following the fire.

I hadn't been there for two days before I set my grandmother's garage on fire, basically burning it to the ground. I still don't know my reasoning for doing that. My unk Jett got in my ass about it though, without ever laying a hand on me. He talked so bad to me that day, it was worse than any ass whopping. Unk had never spoken to me with such anger and piercing words, so it was cutting me to the bone. He ended his verbal assault by saying,

"Hey man, you mad!?"...

"I dig it!"...

"But you can't go around fuckin up everybody else shit!"...

"We players, nigga!"...

"We don't do no punk shit like that!"...

"Doing shit like that is for them low life ass niggas!"...

"That shit ain't even in yo blood boy!"

After unk's psychological ass whooping, setting something on fire never crossed my mind again. Behind all that, he took me inside the house and taught me to tie a tie.

My grandmother's address is the address that's on my birth certificate, so Oakdale is my original roots. Her house was a safe house and the go to spot for everybody. There were a couple of my cousins, an aunt and one of my mother's younger brothers living there. But there were a lot of other family members that were in and out. My granny had twelve children and they were tight knit, so their children grew up together like brothers and sisters. Most of them were boys, so I had a platoon of cousins that were like brothers. Many of them were older than me, but I hung with them like I was their age. They all looked out for me.

I had two younger cousins/brothers and I'll call them Bing and Blue for the sake of the story. We spent a lot of time together. Their father, my mother's brother, was good friends with my father. Our fathers were doing time for the same related incident. We would get into a little bit of everything growing up. We roamed the city, and we came and went as we pleased. We never had a curfew in our life. We were men in boy bodies. Four of my cousins/brothers Shaft, Solo, Dash and Beef all moved to the metro Detroit area at a young age. Shaft, Solo and Dash's mother would come and get me to spend time with them during Christmas break, Spring break and maybe like a month during summer break when I was younger.

Dash and I were closer in age, and we would grind every day whenever I visited. During Christmas break we would go and shovel snow and during summer break we would go and wash cars. We would hit Hungry Howie's up afterwards. Once I saw a group of cats at Hungry Howie's that were fly from head to toe, and they just looked like money. Dash told me they were from Young Boys Incorporated. I had heard a lot about Young Boys Incorporated, so to see some in person with the jewelry and silk suits, pulling out big wads of cash to pay for their food was fascinating to me.

I had a cousin/brother named Raw Dawg. His father was a very powerful well-respected businessman and a huge influence and important piece to our family. He's the man responsible for introducing the game of golf to our family. The first time that I saw a computer was at unk "G's" house back in the early eighties. He had an intercom system throughout his house. I would always sleep in one of the guest bedrooms in the basement whenever I spent the night. In the mornings I would be woken up by the sound of his voice saying,

"Get up and come get ya breakfast."

I heard that repeatedly through the penetrating intercom system. It sounded much like you were being paged at a grocery store or supermarket. Unk used to pay you big money for good report cards. A's were worth $20.00, B's were worth $10.00 and you couldn't wait to see unk "G" on report card day. For somebody in elementary school that was a hell of a lick. I'm sure he probably paid the high schoolers a little more. Raw Dawg's father passed away at an early age. It was a huge loss for Raw Dawg and the entire family. We both ended up living with our grandmother.

Raw Dawg always had that fly prep shit in his closet. I would rock his shit to school even though it was too big for me. I had two cousins/brothers DQ and Red Man who lived maybe four or five blocks from my grandmother's house. I spent a lot of time at their house with them too. Red Man used to do a lot of the sports shit with me, Bing and Blue. He'd have us do football drills; basketball drills the whole nine yards. He spent a lot of time with us. DQ used to keep my hair buttered. I want to say he gave me the first high top fade in the city. He had a huge influence on the younger cousins/brothers.

DQ and Red Man had an older brother Big Dirty who ended up living with me at my grandmother's house too. He was a gorilla in the streets. He always referred to the streets as the concrete jungle and was good with his hands. I have witnessed him do some men so got damn bad that it would leave gashes in their face like they were hit with pipes or sticks. I remember feeling bad for some of them. Big Dirty would hit licks and come in and wake me up in the middle of the night. He would have all types of shit like two or three different kinds of cereals, donuts, cookies and a gallon of milk. He would go and get us two big ass bowls and sit them on the coffee table. It would be quiet as hell while we were sitting there eating. He wouldn't really say much except,

"Get what kind you want."...

"Put some of those donuts and cookies in a bag for school tomorrow."

I attended a private school for the first five years of elementary school. During the third year, I remember attending the class Halloween party. My costume consisted of a pair of cowboy boots, slacks, mock neck shirt and my unk's Dayton Fur Felt Fedora Dobbs hat. The teacher went around the classroom asking the students what they were for Halloween. When she made it to me, I boldly said,

"I'm a pimp!"

I'll never forget the expression it left on her face. I'm the same student that she was taking to McDonald's every report card period for a student and teacher lunch. Back then teachers would often reward their top performing students with kind gestures like that. Nevertheless, I realized that I had poked at her emotions. So, I walked up to her desk to tell her that I was J.R. Ewing, the character from the television series "Dallas" just to make her feel better. Her changed facial expression showed that it did relax her feelings, even though J.R. Ewing's character was worse than any pimp that I had ever seen. She immediately announced to the class what my new costume was.

To this day I never knew who took care of that private school tab, but whoever it was I truly want to thank them from the bottom of my heart. I eventually ended up graduating in sixth grade from Oakdale Elementary. My grandmother and my mother's youngest sister dressed me in a tuxedo for my sixth-grade graduation. I don't recall the number of academic awards I received that day, but it was quite a few to say the least. During my brief stint at Oakdale Elementary I tutored and explained the process of division to a young man who the teacher had written off and given up on. Basically, she told him that he'd never get it. That young man eventually became a superintendent of a public school district and a Giant's Award recipient of his city.

8o's

Back then my granny used to love to play bingo and a few of the bingo halls didn't allow adults to bring children with them. On a few of those occasions, whenever there were no family members available, granny entrusted a young lady to babysit me while she went to play bingo. The young lady would be babysitting a couple of other children, but they were much younger than me. They were like toddlers, it seemed like I had to be like maybe six or seven. I know that I was no older than eight. The very first night she babysat me became my first experience with a woman.

I remember sitting on the couch watching TV while she got up to walk the younger kids into a back room. She went into the room fully dressed then came back out without the kids in a baseball jersey style nightgown displaying her shapely well-proportioned figure. I could see the imprint of her breast nipples through the fitting nightgown, my manhood stiffened up quickly. She sat on the couch right next to me giving off the scent of baby powder with a hint of that old Royal Crown hair grease.

It started by her touching my hair and saying,

"Boy you know you got some good hair!"

Then she kissed my forehead, I guess she was testing the waters to see how I would react. I accepted the kiss because I thought that I was supposed to. She stood up just enough to lift the nightgown to her waist exposing her pubic hair, then sat down and sort of leaned back on the couch. I'm looking at this young lady with this mature body sending my hormones off the chart. She grabbed my wrist guiding my hand between her legs, I could feel the coarse pubic hair and the warm moisture of her pussy on the back of my hand. Using my hand to massage herself, making these soft moaning sounds while gyrating her hips. Eventually she lifted the nightgown up over her large breast encouraging me to kiss one, so I did. Then she requested that I do it again, but this time showing me where she wanted me to kiss on it. Softly palming the back of my head with one hand, I heard a low rough grunt then she kind of moaned,

"Mmmmm, yeah, don't stop!"

With a panting voice while she continued to pleasure herself using my hand.

This happened on a couple of more occasions, each involving intercourse. She was the first to do it, but she wasn't the last. There were two other young women quite older than me in the neighborhood's surrounding district, who I experienced similar encounters with. But because I was raised up under the influence of older men game tapping their conversations, I was thinking that this was what a man was supposed to do. So, in my mind I'm doing man duties not realizing that I was being molested. One day I was with Red Man and Raw Dawg, we were all walking up to Oakdale Elementary to hang out and shoot some ball. I heard them discussing something about some young ladies that they were planning to hook up with later that day. Interrupting their conversation, I blurted out,

"I bust a nut in this girl last night!"

Both of them immediately burst out screaming laughing running around in circles. One of them said,

"Where this lil nigga come from man!?"

They thought I was just talking shit. I just laughed it off with them and even to this day we've laughed about me being so young saying something like that. Although at the time I wasn't old enough to ejaculate, they had no idea where the statement stemmed from or what I had been experiencing.

I lived with my grandmother for much of my life, but I spent a lot of time with my mother's youngest sister when I was younger too. She would take me to hang out with her a lot when I was little. This was before she even had children of her own. I remember when she had her first daughter "Deikh" she was my little sister too. We developed a very close relationship growing up, I could trust Deikh with anything. Even when I became older, my mother's youngest sister was there for me, but we'll get into that a little later.

I learned a lot living with my granny. I was under so much tutelage of game with my granny being the professor of them all. She fed me with so much game that I was more advanced than I ever realized. Granny never withheld information from me. She would always give it to me straight with no chaser. I'll never forget the time she was attempting to wake me up for school one morning, and I didn't wake up right away. She may have called my name like three times, and finally she just yelled out,

"You ain't gone be shit!"...

"Cause the people that want something out of life, they get up and get out!"

It hurt my heart to hear her utter those words to me. Mind you, I couldn't have been no older than 8 years old and I promise you that from that day forward she never had to wake me up for school ever again. I've been getting myself up and getting out ever since. I started hustling candy for a local institution that was known as the Michigan Youth Club. They would drive us to suburban areas and give us a box of candy and send us to go door to door to trade it. I earned well trading candy; it has always been a good feeling to me to be able to buy things and to do for myself. It was a feeling that I fell in love with early in life.

My granny made sure that as a young boy I had a full understanding of my mother's situation and my father's situation. She communicated with me like I was an adult, treating me like a little man. I was so serious at a young age with the aura of a grown man that it earned me the nickname "Uncle Bunts" from my uncle Shang who you'll learn more about later. The name "Boonce" is derived from "Bunts". During the time I was living with my grandmother my mother was still trying to fight her way back from addiction.

My granny used to have family members drop me off at the Bulloch House on Eastern Ave. and Cherry St. to visit my mother every Sunday. It was a Project Rehab building. I would have dinner with my mother, and it seemed like it was always Kentucky Fried Chicken. We would play pool and foosball, and despite the circumstances it was always a good time with her. I loved seeing her clean, healthy and with a sober mind. She would get clean and come get my sister and I to live with her. This would happen periodically, but that got damn addiction is a hell of a thing.

I was young in the mix, taking care of a lot of business with my mother. We used to make quite a few moves together. I've seen and learned a lot of shit hanging with her. She put me up on the game early, supplying me with the basics and fundamentals. I've been hands on since I was like five or six years old. I was so game conscious at a young age I knew about the trick and their purpose in the game's circle of life. I understood that the duties of the hoe was to service the trick, and although I knew what that boy (heroin) was, it always spoked me when I was little. I knew every piece on the board and how each piece moved. I witnessed all of the above firsthand.

I must give the credit for knowing how to drive a car at the age of nine or ten years old to my mother. I was super young when she used to sit me on her lap and let me steer the car while she operated the gas and the brakes. My people were giving me car keys at like ten or eleven years old, sending me on errands and store runs. My driving skills had become so superb that both of my grandmothers were comfortable with having me transport them to the grocery store and pay bills.

There were times that I would make a move with my mother, and she would try to rationalize the reason we were doing what we were doing. Then I would blow her mind with some of the shit that I used to say afterwards. My responses would basically be justifying her reasoning. She would just laugh at me and say,

"Boy don't talk like that."

Everything that we did stayed between her and I. That was one of the first rules that I learned, keep your mouth shut. I witnessed my mother struggle with that addiction shit for years, but she always did good when she could.

All the while my father was sending me letters regularly from the penitentiary. All his letters ended with the saying,

"Everybody got a mellow and you're mine!"

He would send me care packages too. The care packages would have anything from new shoes, watches, clothes, handmade crafts like wooden banks, custom belts, and all kinds of shit. I remember he sent me some all-leather Dr. J Converse with a watch with a leather band. You couldn't tell me shit.

It all seemed regular to me at the time, but as I got older, I wondered how he was locked up and still doing all of that. He would have his younger sister bring me to visit him. Those visits were everything to me. He would be fly as hell every time I would come to see him. He ended up marrying a nurse that worked for the prison where he was locked up. She was the coolest white lady I ever met in my life to this day. My father had her come and get me one summer and take me to Connecticut with two of her sons. I'll never forget that summer. We spent most of our time on a boat on the water. It was a dope ass experience.

Some years passed by, and I was at my granny's house sitting at the coffee table doing my homework. I heard some commotion outside, so I got up and stepped into the doorway of the front door. My grandmother's front door would always be wide open with no screen door attached. I saw the back end of a new Lincoln, so I stepped out onto the porch. The people that were outside were still making noise like they were celebrating. By the time I made my way to the stairs of the porch, I saw a big afro rising out of the car. When I saw the face, I realized it was my uncle "H". He had made it back home from the penitentiary and I was happy as hell to see him. He was Bing and Blue's father.

Unk didn't waste any time at all either. He went and copped a new Cadillac Seville plus a new Cadillac Fleetwood Brougham. Let's just say things changed when he made it back. He bought a pickup truck too, and he would get all the nephews together and take us fishing and camping on a regular basis. He created study hours for Bing, Blue and me. All that shit was fun to me, he made an everlasting impression on me, and he was a major influence in my life.

Not long after Unk touched down, my father's younger sister came to my grandmother's house to get me. We rode out to Kentwood where my father's older sister lived. I didn't think anything of it, because like I said, my aunt would come and get me from time to time. But when we made it out to my other aunt's house and walked in, I immediately saw my father sitting in the living room. My got damn heart dropped to my waist. I was happy as hell to see my father on the other side of those walls.

My old man didn't waste any time either. He went and copped two Mercedes Benz. He bought an E Class and a S Class. It was always rumored that my father and uncles had money hidden or buried somewhere. My father didn't move back to Grand Rapids. He was maneuvering in between Lansing and Jackson, and I would hang with him during spring and winter breaks and sometimes for a few weeks during the summer.

My godfather was released to a halfway house in Lansing. Some days my father would go to meet with him at this park to play tennis. They would hang at that park all day until like thirty minutes or so before my godfather's curfew. I would sit there, and game tap their conversations, my godfather would be going over his blueprint of what he had designed for when he was released from the halfway house. Not too long after those visits in the park, he was officially released, and he didn't waste any time either. He manifested everything that I heard him talk to my father about in those conversations. My godfather purchased a Cadillac Eldorado and a Cadillac Seville that was damn near identical to my unk "H" Seville. I had already bought into the theory of them having money stashed or buried somewhere, but that solidified it for me. There wasn't a soul on earth that could convince me otherwise.

They were all back together on the outside, but then a horrific incident occurred. My godfather was met with a terrible fate when this guy couldn't accept the game. The guy's woman chose my godfather, she no longer wanted to be with the guy. He couldn't stomach that, so one late night-early morning he flashed his headlights flagging down my godfather. The Seville pulled over, and my godfather got out and stood by the passenger side of the car, he was being driven around by his brother. The guy parked behind them and approached my godfather. The two of them began to converse, at some point the guy pulled a pistol out of his pocket and fired the gun multiple times killing my god-father in cold blood. During the course of the altercation, the guy saw my godfather's brother get out of the car and turned and shot at him. He was hit and then fled the scene on foot, managing to survive the ordeal. It was a critical time; all the families were on high alert. The guy was arrested two days later after a shoot-out with police in which one police officer was killed. The tragic event sent shock waves through our families and through the city.

During that time, I was still living with my grandmother on Oakdale St. It was not too long after my uncle "H" got out before he got into another situation that caused him to get back on the run. I wasn't sure what had transpired, but one thing is for cer-tain, my uncles and cousins are the last people on earth that you wanted to violate. So, Unk was back on the run, and I remember him sneaking back into Grand Rapids one night. Somebody must have tipped the authorities that he was back in town, because they almost got Unk that night. I heard that he had to spend a night in a sewer to make his getaway.

I didn't see him for a while after that night. Then one summer he sent for Bing, Blue, Dash and me. We spent that entire summer in Milwaukee, WI. It was one of the most interesting summers I've had to this day. It was an action-packed summer. We ran wild throughout the city. We were having our way with women twice our age. At the time our ages ranged from 10 to 13 years old with Dash being the oldest. I'm not lying when I tell you we were advanced for our age. It was the first time I met "Cuz " who was our cousin that was raised in Milwaukee. "Cuz " was cool as a fan, and he had mad game. My uncle "Bay" was there too that summer on military leave. I hadn't seen him in years. He joined the Army and left Grand Rapids when I was young. Uncle "Bay' was a fly money getting man too. The Jordan 1's had just hit the market and my uncle "Bay" and my uncle "H" pieced together and put a pair on my feet. Bing, Blue and Dash already had a pair on their feet.

The summer had started winding down. I remember all of us dropping off uncle "Bay" at the airport to return for duty. I was sad as shit about that too. I swear about a few days later we woke up one morning and all my uncle "H" closets in the house were empty. Something transpired and he had to get out of dodge again and make another move. I damn near cried that morning and came close to doing it too. My older cousin/brother "Bell" who was the oldest of my grandmother's grandchildren drove us back to Grand Rapids that morning. He had a Lincoln Town Car, and it was like sitting in a living room. I assumed that Bing, Blue and Dash were feeling the same way I was feeling, because that was a quiet ass trip back to Michigan. It was so quiet you could hear a church mouse piss on cotton.

I made my way back to Grand Rapids and I'm just floating around at this time. I'm spending a little time everywhere with my grandmother's house on Oakdale St. being my base. I started spending a lot of time with my cousin/brother on my father's side of the family. His father was my father's older brother "Gip". His name was "Ski" and he had not too long moved from Wyoming to Grand Rapids. His situation had become very similar to mine. I would stay at his mother's house with him for a stint and he would stay at my mother's house with me for a stint. Ski and I created a brother-like bond during that time. We started rapping and performing in talent shows back then. I can remember riding our bikes out to the big stores and stealing all types of shit.

We were hanging so tough that Ski became family to my cousin/brothers on my mother's side of the family. It was one time Dash came to visit and me, him and Ski were walking around the city with intentions of getting chose (picked by a girl). Dash could knock them off too. We were walking down Franklin St. and bumped into my father's first cousin "Bimmy" from Minnesota. My father's uncle owned a house on Franklin St. My cousin Bimmy was a high roller. He had an Excalibur car which at the time I thought was a Rolls Royce. Dash said,

"You must own Perry Drugs or something!?"

He let us all sit in his Excalibur and draped us in "Truck jewelry" gold chains with big ass medallions dangling on them. It's funny because we all thought he was going to let us have the gold chains. We sat in the car calling ourselves appraising the jewelry coming up with a ballpark estimate of how much money we could get if we sold them. After sitting in the car for about 30 to 45 minutes daydreaming, Bimmy came back to retrieve his jewelry and to talk with us and gave us some game to walk with. Even though we were mad about having to return the jewelry, it was a motivating and inspiring moment for me, and I'll never forget it.

Around that time Bing, Blue and I used to grind up money by taking bottles back to get the return deposit or whatever it would take to buy Greyhound tickets to go and visit our cousin/brother Red Man at Michigan State University. Just so happened the Greyhound had a drop off location directly behind the apartment building he stayed in. We would stay no longer than a weekend whenever we did visit. We attended all types of college parties. Although we were on Red Man's watch and his name already carried weight on campus, we earned our respect among some of the OGs from Flint, Detroit, Saginaw and a lot of other cities too. One of the guys from Detroit told us that he had been to Grand Rapids before, and I asked him,

"You been to Grand Rapids and ain't never heard of a nigga named Boonce!?"

Red Man thought that was the funniest shit in the world, he still talks about it today. There were a few other occasions that Dash and I visited the college campus as well. Each of those times there were some young ladies smuggling us into their female dormitory. We were some young live wires. But yeah, we got a chance to experience college life at a young age minus the academic schedule.

Another school year had come and gone, and summer break had made its way back. My uncle "H" had sent for us again. Dash didn't make this trip. Bing, Blue and me found ourselves in Kentucky in the Newport, Covington and Florence area that summer. We spent a lot of time in Cincinnati, OH that summer too. As a matter of fact, it was the first, but not last time that we attended the Kool Jazz Festival which became an annual thing for our family.

One year we did our annual Cincinnati Kool Jazz trip and unk was living in Milwaukee. Unk drove the Benz down there. We met our cousin/brother Red Man and our uncle "D" (one of my uncle's childhood friends) and his sons in Cincinnati that year. We stayed at the Clarion Hotel in the heart of downtown. Back then the Clarion Hotel was crème de la crème. We had rooms on the top floor of that joint. Uncle "H", uncle "D" and our cousin/brother Red Man were hanging out after the concerts every night. Bing, Blue, me and uncle "D" sons were showing out in that hotel. The hotel and the entire downtown were flooded with people. The pool parties at the hotel were going crazy and lasting to the early morning hours. We were all carrying around our own bottle of champagne. It was around three or four in the morning, and we saw our OGs coming up the escalators calling it a night and we were headed down the escalators going back by the pool and into thick of things. Our OGs are still laughing about that to this day. It seems like we ate up a lot of highways during the summer months traveling. It was always a blast being with unk and we did our thing that summer as usual.

I made my way back to Grand Rapids maybe like a month or so before school started. I was at my grandmother's house on Oakdale St. when I heard that distinct Mercedes Benz horn blow outside. Back then Mercedes Benz horns were different from other car horns. I knew it was my father, because that was his routine whenever he would pull up. At this time, he had bought a new Mercedes Benz, and that boy was hardcore. I didn't know it, but he came to take me shopping for school. The Jordan 2's had just dropped, and he put a pair on my feet. After shopping we went over to my other grandmother's house (his mother). He would always give me the keys and let me drive his Mercedes

Benz while he visited my grandmother and his siblings. He's the one who taught me how to drive a stick shift. I would bend a few blocks flexing around the immediate neighborhood.

When he dropped me back off at my grandmother's house on Oakdale St., he slid me a crispy one-hundred-dollar bill. I pinched off that hundred-dollars until damn near to Christmas time. When the school year started, I was the man rocking the Jordan 2's through the hallways. Plus, I had an all-white Nike Air sweatsuit with the black and red Nike on the chest. There was no doubt that it was my favorite outfit. My father took me to a Pistons vs Bulls game that year. Pops bought tickets that damn near put us on the floor. Our seats were not far from the court at all. I wore that outfit and when we walked past the court during a missed free throw, Isiah tapped Jordan then pointed at my shoes and Jordan just looked at Isiah and kind of smiled. I can't explain how that made me feel.

Somewhere during this timeline my uncle Shang was back on the scene. Now my uncle Shang was a got damn mastermind. He was the type of man that would walk around in overalls and a plain white t-shirt with ten thousand in each of his pockets. I never knew where he was during all those years. I don't think he was locked up though. I used to hear that he had some beachfront property down in Florida. But when he finally came back to Grand Rapids, he pulled up in a green Ninety-Eight Oldsmobile with Mississippi tags on it. He had gotten married and had two children. Bing, Blue and I spent a lot of time with him too. He would take us fishing and do all types of shit with us.

I remember we were roaming the city one day and unk road down on us. It was Bing, Blue, Dash, Ski and me. Unk was hanging drywall and doing some carpentry work at a building that he had purchased that was planned to be a future church. He was furnishing and providing a church house for a local pastor. He needed some day laborers, so he came and found us. Unk explained it all to me that day while we were helping him. He broke down the details of shell corporations and non-profit organizations to me that day. He explained in detail how the money goes in and how it comes back out. I knew exactly then what he had created. He shared some valuable game with me that day. Like I say, unk was a mastermind and he was extremely book smart. He also would host fundraisers for his non-profit organization, and we would assist him with those fundraisers as well.

The first one he ever did was at Franklin Park using Barbeque to raise funds, but polish dogs weren't the only thing being traded that day. He would "raise" a boat load of money at these fundraisers. Later that evening we were sitting on the porch drinking Miller Highlife soaking up some game from him. Our OG's allowed us to do a little drinking, cuss and do all types of other shit, and that's probably the reason why I never felt any peer pressure from anybody my age. I've had the greenlight my entire life to do whatever it was that I wanted to do, I never knew what a curfew was. But unk was always against us using any type of drugs. When I was younger before he had to leave, me and Dash walked down in the basement at our grandmother's house, and a few of them were down there smoking weed and drinking beer. Unk Shang called us both over to him, extending his arm with a joint pinched between his fingers. He said,

"Here, hit this."

I walked over to him and leaned forward puckering my lips, preparing to inhale the smoke from the tip of the damn near perfectly rolled joint. Before my lips could touch the joint, unk caught me with an openhanded slap to the side of the head. That's when I heard him yell,

"Don't ever accept dope from no muthafuckin body!"...

"Not even me!"...

"You understand!?"

Stunned from the slap I nodded my head yes. He then placed the joint next to a beer that was already on the table, pointed at them both and said,

"Look man!...

"Ya see this shit!?"...

"It don't have no brain, legs or arms!...

"It can't come to you!"...

"You gotta go get it!"

That game was soaked up immediately, I understood him completely. Let me tell you, I didn't touch weed until I was like twenty-one years old and smoked it until I was like twenty-five or twenty-six years old. It was a short-lived experience for me.

I got the chance to experience a side of unk that many didn't get to experience. Because when he was in business mode, he was a very serious man with a zero tolerance for nonsense. You better not owe him any money. I've seen what happened to people who owed him money but weren't trying to pay. After I would witness him handle those types of situations, he would always say to me,

"It ain't about the money, it's the principle!"

Some bad business had been conducted between unk and some of his Cuban associates. It had to have been a serious matter because he assembled a small army of my uncles and older cousins, equipped them all with high power firearms. Positioned them in strategic locations surrounding my grandmother's house. She was sent away to one of my aunt's houses during the ordeal. I learned of the situation by walking into one of unk's booby traps. One of my uncles yelled out at the top of his voice,

"That's Boonce!"

Unk Shang instantly came to escort me into the house, placing me on the floor beneath a window piling bed covers over the top of my body. He instructed me not to move until he gave me word to. I would hear unk give orders and random gun fire periodically throughout the night. It was a sleepless night, unk eventually relieved my other uncles and cousins of their posts shortly after sunrise. I had no idea what had taken place that night, but I assumed an agreement between unk and his Cuban associates had been ratified. The art of war should have been one of his aliases.

Unk was a highly intelligent street and book smart man. It was a privilege and a blessing to have had the opportunity to have him breathe on me. It's so much game that he had given me at such an early age. He was another major influence in my life. I wanted to be like all of them, so I combined it into one and came out as what I am today. If it wasn't for people like my mother, father, aunts, and uncles I probably wouldn't have ever tried to have shit in life. They all inspired me and made me want to be something and have something. I've always seen that lifestyle on every level, I spent every inch of my life in the game in some shape, form or fashion.

I believe it was that following spring break that my father came to Grand Rapids and took Ski, Dash, me and my cousin Top Cat (my father's youngest sister's son) back to Jackson, MI with him. We hung like wet clothes over there floating in between Jackson and Lansing. I remember there was a man that knew my father who was managing a store in Jackson. When we stepped in the store the man recognized who my father was, and he praised my father the entire time we were in the store. He immediately insisted that we get any and everything that we wanted. Now you know that you can't tell no youngsters anything like that. When I tell you that we didn't hold him up that day, it was like we were on a shopping spree up in there. We took all kinds of shit out of that store. I know we had to leave a few of those shelves empty. See shit like that would happen quite often whenever I would be with my father or uncles.

I received some valuable game from my father. The man had a Mack hand like no other. They broke the mode when they made him. I watched how he maneuvered even when he was still on papers. But when he finally got off parole, it was like he became a different man. He became a "Bubblegum Red 2.0". He started making plays back and forth on interstate 96 east and west, and even started moving east and west on interstate 94. He bought a new Benz every year and kept at least two of them with some type of jeep in his lineup. Although I was right there and witnessed all my father's moves firsthand, he didn't want me to get involved with the life. My father wasn't moving dope either. He never touched dope again after leaving the penitentiary. Like I say, my father was a bona fide Mack. He had three more children after being released from prison, blessing me a little brother and sister in Jackson, MI and a little sister in Milwaukee, WI.

School was letting out for the summer and Bing, Blue and I made our yearly trip to go and hang out with their father. Milwaukee was the spot for us that summer. It was another live summer too. That's when I learned the concept of counting out fifty 20-dollar bills to make a thousand stack, and all the heads of Mr. Andrew Jackson had to be facing in the same direction. Let's just say we counted a lot of 20-dollar bills and made a lot of thousand stacks with the heads facing in the same direction. I was very young when I became comfortable and accustomed to being around large sums of money. It ignited a fire in me that I am still consumed by. I've been in the grips of an obsession to accu-mulate and possess large sums of money ever since.

Unk had bought a new motorcycle that summer and he would let me ride it, but that was until one day he caught me gunning it coming through the alley. I never saw the keys to that motorcycle again, although I still had access to any of his cars that I wanted to drive. Believe me when I say Bing, Blue and I used to get around, man we used to get around Milwaukee. Unk had plans on taking us to Disney World that summer. But he asked Bing, Blue and me if we'd rather go to Disney World or go buy three pairs of any gym shoes we wanted. Now for us that was a no-brainer, give us the shoes, the hell with Disney World. We were on the prowl up and down Interstate 94, the quest to find the hottest gym shoes on the planet. The whole day was spent in Chicago sneaker shopping before we found the exclusive kicks that we wanted. When we made it back to Grand Rapids, we had something really heavy on our feet. The people in our neighborhoods had never seen the kicks we had brought back. There was no store in Grand Rapids that sold the kicks that we had. Uncle "H" didn't want to drive us all the way back to Grand Rapids, because he was trying to avoid the risk of being there. Our cousin/brother "DQ" met us close to Kalamazoo somewhere on Interstate 94 east. When"DQ" saw our gym shoes, it tripped him out. He was a sneaker head too with an exquisite taste, so he could really appreciate them.

It was the start of another school year, and my sneaker game was crazy. When you're at that age those shoes are like cars for you. If Boonce didn't have anything else at that time, he had some fly ass kicks. Coming back to Grand Rapids was always the same ole same ole. I was back to bouncing around from spot to spot, but my granny's house on Oakdale St was always my home base. Even with all the movement and lack of stability, I still managed to maintain a high G.P.A. in school. I credit my grandmother for my shine in my academic achievements.

She was a walking dictionary; she was Google before Google. My grandmother programmed strong reading and study habits in me. Reading was at the top of her list, she would always say,

"Whatever you do, don't stop reading even if it ain't nothing but the newspaper."

When she purchased that set of encyclopedias from those door-to-door salespeople it wasn't just for show. Every book, the entire alphabet from A to Z, was utilized at my grandmother's house. Whenever I asked her certain questions pertaining to my homework, she would always suggest that I research and explore an encyclopedia first. That just didn't go for me, but for anyone that was there.

Every year after my OGs got out, I started basically spending my Christmas breaks and spring breaks with my father and summer breaks with my uncle "H". Those getaways were everything to me. It was like I was recharging my battery. That was pretty much my routine over the next few years. Another summer came and you know what that meant. Uncle "H" sent for Bing, Blue and me. We were in Milwaukee again. I might have been headed to high school that coming fall or just finishing up my high school freshman year. Unk added a new Mercedes Benz and a new Cadillac Fleetwood to his fleet of cars, and I had access to them all.

My uncle Shang was visiting Milwaukee a lot that summer. I thought I was counting a lot of money the prior summer, but this visit I started seeing more money than I had ever seen in my life. One day my uncle Shang told me to drive him to the airport. Bing, Blue and I dropped him off at the O'Hare International Airport. I remember driving the three of us back on that stretch of Interstate 94 West to Milwaukee, driving my uncle "H" Cadillac Fleetwood. I used to push that big boy too. I could barely see over the dashboard in that Fleetwood, but I handled the wheel like I was six feet tall. It's a wonder we didn't get stopped by the police with those three baby faces traveling on the Interstate. But it was nothing for me though, because I had been doing shit like that on a regular basis for a long time. Ever since I can remember, I have been entrusted with grown man responsibilities.

That summer had come and gone as well as a lot of other things. I was back in Grand Rapids, but only for like a week max. My mind was made up, I didn't want to live in Grand Rapids any longer. I picked up the phone and called my uncle "H" to ask him if I could come and live with him in Milwaukee. When unk answered the phone I said,

"I need a favor."

Unk said,

"Yeah, what's up?"

There was a slight pause then I asked him,

"Can I come live with you?

Unk said,

"Hell yeah!"

With no hesitation, almost as if he had been waiting for me to ask him that. So, he sent for all three of us. We didn't all go back to Milwaukee at the same time, we arrived on different days. My uncle Shang had driven my uncle "H" Fleetwood to Grand Rapids like a week or so earlier on some business. So, my mother and I drove it back to Milwaukee and that's how I got back there. It was her, me and my uncle Shang eldest son little "G". He was named after my cousin/brother Raw Dawg's father. "G" had to be around 3 or 4 years old. I doubt if he even remembers taking that road trip. Bing and Blue surfaced like a day or two later.

My uncle "H" enrolled me and Blue in Washington High School. Bing was younger so he enrolled him in John Muir Middle School. Milwaukee was a different culture from what I was accustomed to, although I had already known that from being there during the summers. But I had never attended school there. Unk had established a relationship with a woman whose name was "Nettie". The lady had game galore, and was graceful with it. She became a mother figure to us, treating us like we were natural born sons.

During my time at Washington High School, they installed metal detectors at the door. There were some real heavy hitters that attended that school at the time. Students had Cadillacs and foreign cars parked outside. The cars that they drove were more expensive than the teachers' cars. I was still too young for a driver's license, but I drove to school every day. Blue and I might pull up in the Cadillac for a couple of days out of the week, like Monday through Wednesday then end the week out in the Benz. That's when I started carrying a briefcase to school every day. I was wearing that heavy silk in the fall, and when winter came around, I rocked full-length furs. If you've lived on either side of Lake Michigan, you know how it gets in the winter. My uncle "H" had a hook up at a local Rite Aid where Blue and I would get candy bars in the bulk and take them back to school and flip them. We were organized with it too and had a mad clientele. I'd sell the big candy bars and Blue would sell the bite size. We were selling that shit like dope, and making money hand over fist, we were never broke. We kept a wad of money.

My uncles always made sure that you earned your keep. They would always say,

"I ain't gone turn you into no poor hustler boy!"

That's a phrase that I've been hearing ever since I was little. I remember cleaning out their cars and my uncles telling me that any money that I found was mine to keep. They would have the small change like quarters, nickels and dimes in plain view, but that paper would be in places a lazy hand wouldn't think to clean. It seems like there were always those types of teaching moments when dealing with them, especially my uncle Shang. My uncle "H" would have breakfast prepared for us every morning, with a selection of gold watches and rings to wear. My G.P.A. at Washington High School was higher than it ever had been during my time attending school. The school counselors were already in talks of an academic scholarship to Purdue. There was a star basketball player who was the only player from the city to be named a McDonald's All-American who eventually earned a scholarship to University of Kansas. I had the pleasure of being paired in some classes with him to assist with academics. They all called me

Michigan and have always shown me mad love. I love Milwaukee to this day.

After a while I started helping unk out with more than just counting money. I imagine as the operation was expanding for him, so was the need for a close helping hand that he could trust. I remember sitting at a dining room table with a mountain of work with the Snow Seals Papers. You had to cover your face with a mask or shirt or something, the shit was that potent. I was nervous as hell because the place we were at had wall to wall carpet. All I could think about was, if I knocked this mountain of work off the table onto the carpet it wasn't no way of getting it back, and that was gone be my ass.

I had that nervous feeling every time I did it too, but luckily for me, I never knocked it off the table. Eventually I started being a little more active. I was doing little shit like drops. I remember carrying like an eighfy under my baseball cap and meeting up with a man at the mall. Everything was working like clockwork and my uncles always rewarded me well. I'm glad that we didn't know about smartphones or social media back then, because it was a time that Bing, Blue and I took pictures with all types of guns, wads of cash along with some other things. It was a blessing that unk's connection at Rite Aid intercepted the film that we dropped off to have developed. Believe me, unk wasn't happy at all about it, and he made sure we got the point. Being young and so fascinated with the lifestyle, we never considered that we were jeopardizing the entire operation, but unk reminded us just how serious it was.

Something had transpired where there was a misunder-standing with some business. An individual had sent an idle threat toward my unk saying he was gone pawn him. That put unk head on the swivel. We were all leaving one of unk spots one night, and at this spot you had to walk down a flight of stairs to get outside. As we got halfway down the stairs, we noticed the silhouette of a man standing outside the door. We hadn't heard the doorbell ring, a knock at the door, or anything. There was another set of stairs at the front of the door that led to a basement or storage area, unk told us to get down and crawl in that space. By this time unk done drew down and was ready to light it up. I guess the man at the door started to realize that something was off, so he yelled out,

"It's me, big dog!"

He told unk that he was trying to ring the doorbell, but it wasn't working. It's good that he made himself known, because it almost didn't end well for him. I just knew that I was going to hear the sound of gunfire filling the staircase.

The whole time that I was living in Milwaukee, I was talking to my father at least two to three times a week on the phone. Although I always loved living with my unk, I've always entertained the idea of living with my father ever since I was a little boy. So, I made the decision to go and live with my father back in Michigan. Unk put me on a flight from Milwaukee to Grand Rapids Gerald R. Ford International Airport. I arrived at the airport in a quarter cut hooded Nanny Goat fur coat carrying my briefcase. I remember getting off the plane and being taken directly into the bathroom by Airport Law Enforcement and the Kent County Sheriff's to be searched.

I imagine that they saw this young black teenager with this corner boy energy and just knew that I was dirty, but all they found in my possession was my school transcripts and a few letters from some young ladies that didn't want to see me leave Milwaukee. My mother and father were waiting at the baggage carousel for me. I didn't even mention the incident with the Airport Law Enforcement and the Kent County Sheriff's, because I knew that my mother would've bugged out and made a scene. We dropped my mother off at my grandmother's house on Oakdale St. then me and my father's next stop was Lansing, MI.

My father had his own spot in Lansing, MI and a spot with his wife in Jackson, MI. He gave me the keys to the Suzuki Samurai Jeep. I was originally enrolled in Everett High School in Lansing, MI, but I ended up attending Northwest High School in Jackson, MI. At that time there were only three or four black families in the entire school and there were some white families that didn't want me there. It was a total culture shock for me, something I could have never been prepared for. I'm still coming to school dressed like I dressed in Milwaukee pulling up in the Suzuki Samurai Jeep, hopping out with the Nanny Goat and briefcase. I'm not exaggerating when I say I fought every other day for the first week. One day after school my father peeped a tear in my shirt and asked me jokingly,

"Damn man, what you do, get in a fight today?"

I told him I had been fighting every other day right after gym class. He asked me if it was the same person and I told him no, it was a different group of white boys every other day. The first few of them looked my age, then they started coming with mustaches and beards and it seemed like them white boys liked to grab, pull and wrestle more than they liked to exchange hands. In my mind I always thought that they were trying to take me off somewhere. There would be other white boys that would come and break it up and push off the other ones, and you could hear them saying "This is some bullshit man!" It was a set of twins that was popular for playing football that would always come to help break it up. They were some real cool ass white boys, rich as shit too.

I had no idea that my father was coming up to the school the very next day. I was called out of Biology class to the principal's office, and when I got to the office, I saw my father sitting in there with the principal and my father had a pair of boxing gloves in his lap. When I stepped into the office my father was telling the principal,

"Go get all the boys that don't like my son being here!"...

"Even go get them old muthafuckas and let's take them all down to the gym!"...

"We can line'em up, put the gloves on'em and let'em all go head up one on one with my son!"...

"Let's get this shit over with!"...

"Cause if this shit don't stop, the gloves gone come off!"...

"It's gone get real ugly around this muthafucka!"...

"What ya'll need to know is that he ain't by his self, he got people too and will tear this muthafukin school up about him!"

I remember the principal's bottom lip was shaking while he was trying to explain to my father that he had no knowledge of any of the incidents, and that he couldn't approve any boxing matches on the school property. I'm not sure exactly what the principal did after that, but we only had stare downs, but there was no more action after that meeting between my father and the principal. My father said,

"That muthafucka knew that that shit was going down!"...

"I saw it in his eyes that the cracker was lying!"

The word had gotten around the school that my father was a gangster, and how I got off on them white boys and held my own with the mustaches and beards those first few days of school. I've never been a violent man by nature, but I was always good with my hands.

As I was saying, it was only three black girls, me and another black dude that attended the school. The other black dude was from the area and was raised around a lot of the locals, and thought he was one of them. I became very close with one of the black girls, she eventually became my woman. She was originally from Detroit, MI, but had moved to Jackson, MI to live with her grandmother. With both of us being in unfamiliar territory we spent a lot of time with each other and found that we had a lot in common. Our upbringing was similar, and she was book smart as hell. We would study tough together. She kept me on my toes with my academics, she used to say,

"Getting a "B" is uncivilized!"

When we first started kicking it, she told me that I was her man way before I even knew that I was her man. She was crazy about me too and would tell me all about how she'd hear how the white girls at the school would be talking about me like I was a rock star, and how she was going to end up having to kick somebody's ass. She told me that's why a lot of those white boys don't like me. But I was hip to it already because the white girls were always shooting their shots, buying, and giving me shit. I accepted all gifts and entertained them, but I never touched any of them because I didn't trust them nor the surroundings. They were buying me shoes, giving me money, all kinds of shit. They made me feel like I was a D1 athlete on my way to school to play ball. One day my father's wife came into my room, saw my shoe collection and told my father that I had more shoes in my room than her three sons had combined in their entire lifetime.

The school year was coming to an end, and I found out that my father and his wife were getting a divorce. My father still had his spot in Lansing, MI, but I chose to go back to Grand Rapids for the summer break. I had gotten my driver license in Lansing before I went back to Grand Rapids, so I'm driving legally now. I would drive over to Lansing to meet up with my woman. We would always meet where US-127 and I-96 connect at our spot-on S. Pennsylvania Ave. She didn't like the fact that I was talking about not coming back to Jackson for the upcoming school year. She'd cry like a baby every time I'd leave to go back to Grand Rapids.

The closer the upcoming school year approached, the less she started hearing from me. The last time that I heard her voice she was talking about moving to Grand Rapids after she graduated high school, and she entertained the thought of me possibly enrolling in the same college that she was planning to attend. She would be a senior that upcoming school year and I would be a junior. Her eyes and heart were already set on Michigan State University, and she had already applied to attend at the end of the school year. It was pretty much a guarantee for her. I was deliberately trying to create distance between us so I would tell her things like,

"I might even be moving back to Milwaukee to finish my senior year of high school,"

That really crushed her. Then she started talking about the possibilities of applying to Marquette University and moving to Milwaukee. She'd call and send letters to my grandmother's house, but I stopped responding after a while. I didn't feel good at all about it, but I knew that the game was changing for me. I'm sure she's a successful woman and doing well today.

90's

Now I was back in Grand Rapids for summer break and my cousin/brother Solo was coming back and forth from the east side of the state at that time. He and my cousin/brother Raw Dawg had something in motion. I already knew what they were doing, I just didn't know what product they had. They were both wearing fly ass sneakers with the Nike and Adidas tracksuits, and the baseball caps pulled low and fitted tight on their heads. He would always come to Grand Rapids in a rental car and one time he drove his customized Chevy S-10. That's when I knew that they were really earning because the shit he had done to that Chevy S-10 wasn't cheap. I cut into him trying to get in on whatever he and Raw Dawg had going on, but they thought it was best that I continued to focus on school and not get involved. They had no clue what I had been doing in Milwaukee.

I'm sitting back watching the dynamics of things changing not only in the neighborhood but in the entire city. I came to learn that a product they called crack was changing lives and little did I know it would change the face of America. When I was in Milwaukee the product was being served soft, so I had never seen crack before. I had heard of it, but never actually saw it. I know people used to free base back when I was younger, but it wasn't like this product. It was said throughout the neighborhood that the house behind us in Milwaukee when we stayed on twenty eighth and Chambers was trading crack. I remember when I lived with my unk, he told me that my cousin/brother Dash had gotten knocked with some crack as a juvenile on the east side of Michigan. That had to be around eighty-seven or eighty-eight when my unk told me that. They assigned Dash to Job Corp. in Grand Rapids. So, he was in Grand Rapids by the time I made it back there for summer break. Job Corp was only letting him out for a few hours out of the day though.

Now I'm trying to figure out what would be my next move. If I was going back to Lansing or even going back to Milwaukee. One day I was sitting on my grandmother's porch just chilling and contemplating on which way I should go. It had to be around the first or the third of the month because my mother came out of the house and gave me sixty dollars from her monthly check. She told me,

"Boy you better get you some of this money."

She was referring to the crack trade. Back then sixty dollars would get you started with a sixteenth. My cousin/brothers wouldn't trade with me at that time, so I went to some people from Detroit that had a house on Oakdale St. who knew and respected my cousin/brother Big Dirty. The product was served to me soft, and my mother put it in a jar of water with some baking soda and cooked it. After it cooled it became hard in the shape of a small crescent moon in a corner of the jar. I used a razor blade to chop it up into pieces. I chopped seven pieces that would retail for twenty dollars each. I traded all seven of them within fifteen minutes. It seemed like every other person that you would see in public would ask you,

"You straight?"

To see if you had some product to trade. I went back down the street to the people from Detroit a few more times that day for the same order. By day's end I had seen over eight hundred dollars. After that first day trading, I was no longer contemplating leaving Grand Rapids, my mind was made up that I wasn't going anywhere. When I learned what Arm & Hammer could do, life as I once knew it, would never be the same. I woke up the next day and stopped by the Detroit people's house, but they were sold out and didn't have anything to trade. They told me to give them a day or two, and they should be back in the pocket. I was keeping what I was doing all to myself and low key.

My uncles nor my cousin/brothers knew about what I was doing at the time. So, while I'm waiting on the Detroit people to restock, I was enjoying the fruits of my labor. I ended up running into an old childhood friend from the Oakdale, Adams, and Evergreen district. He had a plastic bag of product that was already chopped into about fifty pieces. He explained to me that it wasn't all his, but it was given to him on consignment, so he wasn't in any position to trade with me. But he did ask me if I wanted to help him trade the product...and I agreed with it. So, I kept thirty dollars from every five pieces that I traded and gave him seventy dollars back. We emptied that plastic bag in no time. He told me he would introduce me to his supplier so that I could do some trading directly, but he never took me to meet them. Although he did come back around with another fifty count, I passed on helping him trade it this time though.

I had a few dollars in my pocket with no one to trade with. I decided to do some early school shopping. I kept all the shopping bags in the back of the Suzuki Samurai Jeep. A few days passed, and word got to me that my father was in town. He didn't know yet that I had made up my mind to stay in Grand Rapids. So, I rode down on him over at my grandmother's house (his mother) just to holler at him. We gave each other dap and started kicking it and he said,

"Man I'm surprised you ain't got the top off the jeep today."

But I didn't have the top off because I had all those shopping bags in the backseat. He started talking about the upcoming school year, and how J.W. Sexton High School and Everett High School were some of the options for me and that would put me around more people who looked like me. We talked about a few other things for a while and then he asked me,

"Do you want to roll over to Lansing with me?"...

"I gotta take care of some business, but I'm coming right back tomorrow."

So, I locked the jeep up and hopped in the Benz with him and took that ride over to Lansing. When we made it back to Lansing, we didn't go directly to the bachelor pad, but we pulled up at this big ass luxurious house with a three-car garage, a real baby mansion. I didn't ask anything, but I was thinking to myself that it was some singer or entertainer's home. Then I thought, shit this could be Magic Johnson house. The driveway had a nice length to it too. As we were driving up the driveway my father said,

"I want to introduce you to a friend of mine."

I was anxious to see who it was too. There was a money green Cadillac Eldorado parked outside the garage area. My father reached over and grabbed a gadget from the glove compartment and pushed a button on it and one of the stalls of the garage started opening.

We entered the house through the garage. You had to walk through a large foyer area that gave you a lounge feel when you entered the house. From there you entered another doorway with an open area that led to the lower level and a short set of stairs that led up to the kitchen. I was like uncle Ice on Paid-In-Full,

"I can smell a muthafucka with money!"

As we made our way into the kitchen. I took a seat at a table that was in the kitchen area and my father continued to make his way through the house to get upstairs. When he returned downstairs there was a white woman accompanying him wearing loungewear and a pair of glasses with burgundy frames. I stood up to shake her hand and to formally introduce myself although my father had already shared our names with both of us. She then asked me if I would like anything to eat or drink and offered to give me a tour of the house. As we were walking through the house, I thought to myself that this is some, "Knots Landing" and "Dynasty" type shit. When we made our way upstairs, she showed me a bedroom that was like an efficiency apartment minus the kitchen. It had a bathroom, lounge and dressing area and a cherry wood desk in it. She started explaining to me that her home was my home and that I was welcome there any time I wanted to come and stay. To this day I never knew what her occupation was. My father and I finished our visit, which turned out to be a very nice visit and we headed back to the bachelor pad.

We woke up the next day and went back to Grand Rapids. In that forty-five-to-fifty-minute ride back to Grand Rapids he dropped some game on me like he never had before. He said,

"Now this might not be the best example but it's the best example"

Then he asked the question,

"What's the hardest thing for a man to master?"

At this time, I'm just looking at him but not saying anything waiting to soak it all up. He said,

"The hardest thing for a man to master is a woman."...

"See that's what make a pimp unique, cause they can master a woman's mind."...

"Very few men have what it takes to be a pimp."...

"And I'm not talkin about accepting money from women for selling their pussy cause that's illegal."..

"This thing is all about knowing the game then taking the game to another level."...

"But you wanna respect the law at the same time."...

"You don't want'em to work the tracks, you want'em to work the fax."

He went on to talk about how pimping was a non-contact sport, it was a game of the mind, and it's played from the shoulders up, ear to ear. Then went on to say,

"Hey player!"...

"In every situation there's a pimp and a hoe"...

"You just want to make sure ya the pimp."...

"Ya godfather used to say",...

"Somebody gotta play the fool."...

"Don't let that be you!"...

"Always keep ya fronts up."...

"Watch how you get chose with ya mouth closed!"...

"You know they quicker to pay that ransom when ya clean and handsome!"...

"Ya understand!"...

"Pimp Red!"

He ended with a loud laugh while simultaneously applying more pressure to the car accelerator. There was so much that he said on that trip, and I didn't know if pops was trying to justify the game that he had just exposed me to or was he trying to tell me that it was the best and safest game to play if I ever decided to partake in that lifestyle. To this day I have kept that game in my back pocket. That entire ride all I was thinking about was where I was going to find some product to trade when I made it back. I still hadn't made any mention of my decision to stay in Grand Rapids for the upcoming school year. We pulled up to my grand-mother's house (his mother) and I went in with him to get some love from my grandmother and to fellowship for a minute.

I hopped in the jeep and went down on Oakdale. The min-ute I parked, I immediately walked down to the Detroit people to see if they had something to trade. They told me I had just missed them, and they didn't have any product to trade. At this point, I started to think that they were lying and just didn't want to do business with me anymore. Everywhere that you'd go people would still be asking the question "You straight?" and all I could think about was the money that I was missing out on. I found myself out at Woodland Mall, not doing any heavy shopping, but if I saw something that I liked I was going to buy it. I stopped in the Merry-Go-Round store and saw a guy I knew from childhood with two fists full of shopping bags. I immediately knew what was up. We shared a little bit of small talk for a minute, then I cut into him about some product. He told me that he didn't have anything to trade, but he know somebody that did.

Come to find out the individual he had in mind was "Rocky". Rocky's mother and my mother were good friends that used to run together back in the day, his mother and my uncle Shang were a couple at one time too. At times, my mother would leave me at their house, and Rocky would watch me for a while and they would go out and make their moves. I told my guy to let Rocky know that it was me, and if it was okay if I got his number and I'll be down on Oakdale. Later that day my guy pulled up on Oakdale to share Rocky's pager number with me, and I didn't delay in paging him. He called back promptly, and we talked for a minute. He asked me what I've been up to, and how my mother was doing and things like that. Then I told him that I was looking to do some trading and how much money I had to invest. He said,

"Man you know yo money ain't no good with me, you family boy!"

He gave me a location to meet up with him. He tested me with a quarter of an ounce on consignment. That was three times the amount of what I started out getting from the Detroit people. The product was soft when I received it, so I found an old friend of my parents to cook it for me. I chopped like twenty-five or twenty-seven pieces from it, each of them retailing for twenty dollars. I gave a piece to the person who cooked it for me. This lady was old friends with my mother, and she was bringing me so much business that in a little of no time, I was paging Rocky so that I could return his share of the earnings. We met up again, and he gave me the same order and it was like Déjà vu because I paged him right back to return his shares. At the third meeting he gave me four times the amount of the original order, which was a whole ounce. I chopped like a hundred twenty to a hundred twenty-five pieces from it, and the pieces retailed for twenty dollars each. I gave the chef three pieces for cooking it, and she went out and recruited even more customers to trade with. Many of the customer base were individuals who grew up and went to school with my OGs, some even remembered me from when I was a baby.

At this time, it seemed like everybody, and their momma were using. The trade was going fast and easy, and I was earning good. My father eventually found out what I was doing. One of the customers saw him in Grand Rapids out and about and approached him about my operation. My father didn't take well to the news. By the time I made it back to Oakdale they told me my father had been there twice looking for me. He left word that he would be at my grandmother's house (his mother) and to come and holler at him. I pull up to my grandmother's house (his mother) and I have no idea that he knows what I've been doing. He wasn't one to beat around the bush, and he came right with it. My father told me that the man said,

"Hey Red, ya'll got that premium shit man!"...

"Ya son is game then a muthafucka too, just like ya'll was!"...

"He got that shit runnin like a candy store over there Red!"

The man assumed that my father was supplying me. My father started stressing to me how serious it was and how it was even bringing heat on him. Heat that he didn't need or want. The conversation had become very tense and everything that he was saying started to fall on deaf ears. That's when I finally broke the news to him about me deciding to stay in Grand Rapids to finish school. He told me that he couldn't continue to let me keep the jeep if I was going to continue to be out here trading, he stated,

"Now that's up to you man!"

But I had my mind made up and there was no convincing me otherwise. I immediately went down on Oakdale St. and had my cousin/brother Raw Dawg follow me back to a house my father was at, which was a lady friend of his that lived in Grand Rapids. I dropped the jeep off to him. The situation put a strain on our relationship to the point that my father even stopped speaking to me.

Now I don't have a car or any wheels to get around with, but I have a decent surplus of funds and a reliable source of product. I kept the same routine with my operation out of the way. This was during a time when Prospect Ave. from Garden St. to Highland St. was overpopulated with traffic. It was like Wall Street, everybody and their mother was trading. But at this time Oakdale St. was slow with very little to no traffic. I was tucked away at the east end, never having to leave the house. I had a recruiter recruiting the customers that were big spenders from Prospect Ave. directing them back to her house. It was all working in my favor.

One night I was chilling at my grandmother's house, and my cousin/brother Raw Dawg's old girlfriend from high school came to pick him up to go bowling. She had her two sisters with her, and I had been wanting to get at the youngest one since Raw Dawg and her sister were kicking it back in high school. They invited me to come along, and I didn't hesitate to hop in the backseat with them. When I got in the car, they both asked how old I was. I gave them some ridiculous young age like 12 or some shit like that. They both knew I was lying, and they both said,

"Mmm"

I knew then she would be mine. We did a little small talk, but really nothing more than that. We all ended up having a good time that night.

Mind you that at that time Raw Dawg didn't have a clue that I was in business. Just so happened he was waiting on Solo to return to Grand Rapids and Raw Dawg had established a crazy clientele that he wasn't able to serve. I had just met with Rocky and restocked my supply that day before we all went bowling. So, I revealed my secret to Raw Dawg and he had bought my entire supply. I guess you can consider that as my first wholesale transaction. I told Rocky that I would be needing more supplies, and he didn't hesitate to provide me with it. A few days had passed and Solo still hadn't made it back, so Raw Dawg continued to buy at least 50 to 60 percent of my supply. This system that I established allowed me to trade product at an alarming rate, and it solidified my business relationship with Rocky. I'd like to believe that I was his top earner at that time.

It was a few of us sitting outside at my grandmother's house and Raw Dawg's old girlfriend and her sister pulled up and called me out to the car. When I got to the car, Raw Dawg's old girlfriend told me that her little sister was digging me, and I looked at her little sister and let her know that I was digging her too. Everything is history after that. I wanted to take her out, but I didn't have a car at the time. I paged my supplier Rocky who had a 1989 Nissan Maxima and remember it was the summer of '89'. I told him that I had met a young lady and wanted to take her out and show her a nice time, but I didn't have any wheels. He knew what I was getting at and before I could get it out to ask him, he had already offered me the keys to the Maxima. The crazy thing is that I didn't have to go and pick it up. He had a lady follow him, and he dropped it off to me.

It was loaded to the T too. It had that soft ass butter leather and a factory stereo system that was sonically superb. I had that

Special Ed "I Got It Made" off that Youngest in Charge album thumping. I had one of the customers go and get me a hotel room in their name. Woodland Mall was my next stop to grab something to wear before I headed to the room to freshen up. I picked up the young lady for dinner and a movie and we enjoyed each other's company that evening. I dropped her off at home immediately following the movie. We sat outside her parent's house, and I talked with her for a while. We both agreed that it was something that we would absolutely do again. I left there and slid back out in the streets to bend a few corners to see what I could get into.

The next morning, I returned Rocky his car and he dropped me back off back on Oakdale St. That's when I learned that Solo was back in town and that he wanted to holler at me. So, I waited there for him at my grandmother's house on Oakdale. He pulled up clowning in a rental car and when he let the window down, he had that Gucci Crew II "They Call Me Gucci" bumping off that "What Time Is It? It's Gucci Time" album. He signaled me over to the car and was turning down the music at the same time. I bent my head over into the passenger side window and we gave each other some dap. He said that he was headed back to the east side of the state and asked if I wanted to ride with him. I told him yeah, but I couldn't leave until later that evening. I still had some product that I needed to trade, and I wanted to settle my balance with Rocky before I took off anywhere. Solo told me that he still had a few more moves to make too so we agreed to meet up at our grandmother's house around seven or eight o'clock that night. I went to work immediately after Solo pulled off and ended up trading all my product sooner than I expected. I paged Rocky to meet up with him and to settle my balance. I let him know that I wouldn't need to replenish my supply at this meeting because I was headed out of town, and I didn't know for how long. Rocky told me not to even worry about that and told me that I was good for it. He urged me to restock before I left but I declined his offer.

Solo pulled up to our grandmother's house a little after seven o'clock. I had put together a few fly garments and my entire earnings inside of a duffle bag just in case we decided to do something. I hopped in the rental and threw the duffle bag in the backseat. Solo had the pager clipped to the sun visor and the brick cell phone resting on the emergency brake in between the driver and passenger seats. He didn't waste any time putting what he wanted to talk to me about on the floor. Before we could get to Interstate 96 east good, he started to mention that he heard that I was in business. He said if I was choosing to be in business anyway, we might as well all do it as a family. He then pitched the idea to me that it would be best if we kept all our business between our grandmother's grandchildren. But his idea was really what I wanted all along, so I was already on board before the conversation even got started. I was always mesmerized by the way my uncles and father worked together and how they had their business organized.

When we made it to the east side of the state, we made a stop at his girlfriend's apartment, and he grabbed a Footlocker bag half filled with money out of the trunk. I knew it was money because I noticed the bumps at the bottom of the bag. We eventually made our way over to my aunt's house (his mother), but she wasn't there, so I didn't get a chance to see her on this trip. We both caught a quick nap that night and woke up early the next morning, took showers and got dressed. We stopped and ate breakfast at a little spot that Solo liked to go to. After breakfast we went to Northland Mall, did some light shopping and when we left there we went over to Greenfield Plaza. Solo copped a Cuban link chain necklace at Greenfield Plaza, and I saw the one that I wanted but it would have put a major dent in my surplus, but I vowed to myself that I was coming back to buy that thing.

Solo was having some more work done to his truck, so we went by the shop that was customizing it. The guy was just about done with it, and he was putting that thing together! When I got to the garage, I noticed that the truck didn't have a top on it anymore. He had converted it into a hardtop convertible. He customized the interior of the cab and the bed with black full-silk velvet with red trim with two bucket seats installed in the bed of the truck. The bucket seats in the bed could lay flat to allow you to zip the rag top material to cover them up whenever it rained. The kit he had put on it was inches from the ground. It had a chrome trim with the words "Strictly Business" on the driver and passenger door and had it in larger letters on the door of the bed. There's no doubt that he created a head turner. Before we got back to Interstate 96 west, we stopped and parked at a car wash, and Solo made a call from the brick cell phone just to say,

"I'm here."

He then ended the call. We sat there for a minute talking about a little bit of everything and then a Mazda MVP minivan pulled up alongside us. Solo got out and walked to the back of the car and opened the trunk. A gentleman got out of the minivan with a towel and box of Tide washing detergent in his hand. He walked to the back of the car where Solo was, when he returned to his minivan, he didn't have the towel or the Tide washing detergent box in his hand. Instead, he was carrying a Nike shoe box under his arm.

We made our way back to Grand Rapids and went directly to one of our cousins/brothers' apartments. Solo brought the Tide washing detergent box in with him. This thing looked like it came off a store shelf, and it opened like a box of new washing detergent too. But once the box was opened it was only enough detergent to cover up what looked like from an eyeball view a quarter slab. We all stayed in the kitchen while he did his chef thing. With that amount of product, it took a little longer than what I had been accustomed to. I watched his cooking method very carefully, step by step. Because I knew it was a skill that I would need moving forward.

I first learned how to cook using a pot of boiling water on top of the stove, but the process eventually evolved to the microwave. Once he was finished, Solo furnished me with a hefty supply of consignment at a more than generous price. So, even after subtracting his share from the gross, my net profit margin was high. This created a hunger in me that increased my greed and ambition for more. The dynamics of business changed for me. Greed encouraged me to join the crowded block of Wall Street trading. I had become a full-fledged corner boy, plus I had a recruiter still rounding up and directing customers my way. Solo always made sure that I had more than enough product. I knew that as long as I kept my tab current he would leave the faucet running.

The school year was set to begin, and I was scheduled to attend orientation for my junior year at Ottawa Hills High School. Solo truck was finished getting customized. He had brought it over to Grand Rapids the week of orientation. So, that's what I drove to the orientation, and I had the hard top off with the seats sitting up in the back. That "Move the Crowd" off that Eric B. & Rakim "Paid in Full" album was banging in it sounding like a live concert. The truck had two twelve-inch speakers in the cab so when I pulled up in the auditorium parking lot, it caught the attention of many of the students, attracting quite a few of them to the windows to see. My mother accompanied me to enroll me in school.

As me and my mother walked through the doors, I noticed Raw Dawg's old girlfriend's little sister standing with her friends. I went over to speak to her and to try to set something up for us later after orientation. I told her I didn't have a car at the time, and she said that was okay, and that she'd come and pick me up. After examining my transcripts, the school administration scheduled me to all advanced classes like trigonometry and shit and I was cool with it. Now my mother has successfully enrolled me, I had my class schedule, and I was ready for the school year. We made our way back down to my grandmother's house on Oakdale, and not long after, I saw a white drop top with three females in it pulling up in front of the house. I recognized that Marie was the driver. Marie was the name of Raw Dawg's old girlfriend's little sister. We just took a ride around the city that day just kickin it.

My junior year of high school had officially kicked off, I had been attending for a few months now. A lot of events had taken place during those few months. My uncle Shang had got pinched and was fighting a case from the inside of a jail cell. Law enforcement raided a hotel room from a tip that they had received. They found product in an empty hotel room and later that day they arrested unk and charged him without him ever being in possession of any product. He hadn't been to the hotel, and he was miles away from the hotel when they decided to take him into custody. Unk hired one of the best criminal defense attorneys in western Michigan to help fight his case.

Meanwhile Dash graduated from Job Corp., and he and I joined forces in the business of trading product on the blocks of Wall Street. Our stocks were increasing rapidly by the day. Ever since we were little, when we were going door to door, washing cars and shoveling sidewalks and driveways, we've always been a great force whenever we teamed up together. The colder months started settling in but the blocks of Wall Street were on fire. We were doing what was called "all nighters" which is nothing more than working a double shift at a job with the second and third shift combined. It had gotten to a point where I would leave directly from the blocks of Wall Street to attend school the next morning. Sometimes I would report to school wearing the same clothes that I had worn the day before. I recall wearing a Used jean outfit two days in a row, and a young lady saying,

"Ugh Boonce had them clothes on yesterday!"

I took both hands and dug down in each of my front pockets and pulled out two wads of money and said,

"But I didn't have these in my pockets yesterday!"

I remember all of the students that were standing around at the time just going crazy after I had said that. Although that wasn't my style, she tried to embarrass me and left me with no other choice but to put her in her place.

During the time I am attending Ottawa Hills High School, I became close with a young man by the name of Big Mac. We had become like brothers, and he became family to my family. Big Mac was a very intelligent and conscious person. A real stand-up guy and I've never witnessed him backing down from nothing or nobody. Before me and him ever built a brother like relationship, there was this one time that me, Bing, Blue and Solo were riding through the city and Big Mac was standing outside of an ice cream shop on the corner of Hall and Fuller. Big Mac yelled out something to me in a joking manner, but they thought that he had said something to me with ill intentions. If I haven't mentioned it already, my family doesn't play when it comes to me. So, Solo pulls the truck over and everybody gets out to address Big Mac. Nothing ever escalated but Big Mac stood his ground during the short-lived ordeal. To this day they've all laughed about that misunderstanding a million times. Big Mac family was a powerful family in the city too with a lot of muscle. Although our families never did direct business together (outside of the business dealings that his nephew and I had later) there was always a mutual respect between the families.

The presence of that Michigan winter was being felt. The snow and that hawk had signed a new lease agreement and was going to be around for a while. Dash and I would go and buy the Carhartt jumpsuits, thermal socks and insulated boots and work the block of Wall Street for two or three consecutive days at a time. Typically, on the third day or so we would have a customer go and get us a hotel room to recharge and to freshen up. We had a good rhythm going and were trading at a rapid pace. We were young and we were living life on our own terms. I don't know if there is any better feeling for a man than to earn his own money independently with the ability to come and go as he pleases.

As if things couldn't have gotten any better, I received word that my uncle "Bay" who was in the military wanted me to give him a call. When I reached out to unk, he told me that the engine in his Audi Five Thousand had blown and that I could have it if I went and picked it up. Unk was buying his cars directly off the show-room floors, so the Audi wasn't but a couple years old. Needless to say, I had the car shipped to a mechanic in Grand Rapids to have an engine dropped in it. I was earning good, and everything was going good during that time, but one Friday night changed that narrative.

Dash and I had hit the blocks of Wall Street to trade as we usually do, and a Grand Rapids Police Department cruiser caught us off guard with an ambush. While we were cutting through the alley, they were sitting in the cut with their lights off. Before we knew it, we were pent-up between the cruiser and the rear wall of the store. This was not normal behavior for the Grand Rapids Police Department at that time, they weren't doing shit like that. But the game had changed, I guess. Dash and I were some of the first combatants of George H.W. Bush's 1989 so-called war on drugs.

They pushed us both up against the cruiser and com-menced frisking us digging through our pockets. They were pull-ing nothing but lumps of money out of Dash pockets all the time asking him where he got it from. I was wearing an insulated air force jumpsuit with zipper pockets all over it. The officers pulled sandwich bags filled with product from many of the different zipper pockets. Two bags were filled with nickels, the other two with dimes and two more filled with twenties. I had planned on trading all of it before the night was over, but the Grand Rapids Police Department canceled those plans. They didn't arrest Dash, but they still put him in handcuffs and took him into custody and because he was seventeen and considered an adult, they took him downtown.

On the other hand, I was arrested and charged with pos-session with intent to distribute. Because I was sixteen, I was still considered a minor and I was taken to the Kent County Juvenile Detention Center. Before taking me to the Detention Center, the officers told me that because I was only a juvenile, they didn't need to do any paperwork on me, that they would drop me off at home if I admitted that I was holding the product for Dash. At that moment I figured out the reason they detained him. I told the officers that Dash had no knowledge of the product that I was in possession of. Because I didn't cooperate, they had to release Dash that night and because it was Friday, I ended up spending the weekend in the Kent County Juvenile Detention Center.

They escorted me directly to a cell upon my arrival at the detention center. Saturday morning, I was escorted to a day room where I saw a few familiar faces. Some of them became notorious men in Grand Rapids. There was a young man that was facing a murder charge, and I knew who he was because it was being published all over the Grand Rapids Press and all the local news TV stations. There was another young man that I grew up with and I knew him very well. He went on to earn a reputation of being a very dangerous man in the city. Today he is serving a life sentence for premeditated first degree murder. Although I have personally never experienced that side of him, because he has always addressed me with the utmost respect and love, and I've always presented him with the same. But the most torturing thing about that entire weekend to me at the time was that I didn't know when I was going home. Not realizing and understanding the law at the time that I was only a juvenile and that I only needed a guardian to be released on the next business day. So, Monday finally came, and I was released to the custody of my mother's youngest sister. My grandmother and her came to pick me up from the detention center. That was the longest weekend I ever experienced. After receiving probation and community service that morning I made a vow to myself that I would never get caught with my pants down like that again.

As part of the conditions of my probation, I couldn't be seen on Oakdale St. at all, and I had to go and live with my mother's youngest sister. She gave me the basement to do as I pleased with it. I made it very comfortable down there. It was basically an apartment. It was a gentleman who was a heavy weight in the city that owned a few car lots that assisted me with completing the community service side of things. Not long after moving in with my aunt my uncle Shang sent me a letter from the penitentiary telling me not to touch or trade any product until he made it back home. I gave ear to unk's instructions, and I laid low. At the time I had a decent surplus of dough saved in two shoe boxes, so I had that to pinch from for a while. I started focusing on getting my Audi Five Thousand on the road and putting it together how I wanted it. So, I got the engine dropped in it, got it painted metallic blue, put the chrome Hammers on it and put the chrome plates on the doors. If I must say so myself, that thing was sitting pretty. Not bad at all for a sixteen-year-old youngster. Dash had bought an Audi five thousand too the same year as mine except his was black.

While I was waiting on unk to make it back home from the penitentiary, Marie and I had started spending a lot of time together and had become very close with one another. She was the type of female that could care less about all the money and the cars and shit. Those things didn't impress her, and I was digging that about her, and it solidified the relationship. There was a gentleman from her prior relationship that didn't take well to the new arrangement. One evening I was riding in the car with Marie on our way over to my aunt's house, and I asked her to ride down Oakdale St on our way there, even though I wasn't supposed to be anywhere near Oakdale St. The traffic light stopped us at the corner of Eastern Ave and Oakdale St facing south on Eastern. I noticed a group of people with loud voices loading into a white van in the parking lot of Willie's corner store. I didn't think much of it, I thought it was some of the homies from the neighborhood, or some of Solo's soldiers that he had brought over from the east side of the state.

As Marie began to make a right turn the taillights on the white van brightened, going from the parked position, to reverse into drive. The block of Wall Street was busy on the east end of Oakdale St that night too. Many of my cousins/brothers were out there trading, I instructed Marie to stop the car so that I could kick it with them for a quick second. No sooner than the car stopped, the white van pulled in front of us, and the group of people unloaded from it. Among them was the gentleman from Marie's prior relationship approaching the car in a very aggressive manner. While all this was taking place my people started coming out of the woodworks from everywhere. They were outnumbered, you couldn't count the number of people standing out there on my behalf. Now we're all standing face to face in the middle of the street by this time unbeknownst to me Dash and Bing had slipped off to retrieve some artillery. The gentleman was acting a little uneasy while sharing a few words. I politely turned to Marie to ask her who she wanted, she then answered,

"I want you."

That answer didn't sit well with him. He attempted to cause a disturbance, and someone said,

"Hey man, that's the game you gotta respect it!"...

"She don't want you no mo!"

Shortly after those words were spoken all you could hear was rapid gun fire. The gentleman and his people all hustled back to the van and proceeded to drive off. Come to find out that Dash and Bing were the ones with the Peacemakers. Big Dirty wasn't in attendance that night, but I'm sure he paid the gentleman a visit after hearing what had transpired. Big Dirty didn't allow an individual to look at me too long.

The snow was melting away, and warmer temps were starting to boguard the days. Just as the spring season made its way back, so did unk. He made his way back home on an appeal bond. He was ordered to house arrest on an ankle monitor at my grandmother's house on Oakdale St. Around the same time, I had successfully completed my probation terms with the juvenile courts, and they dismissed the alleged charges, and the case was closed. I started spending a lot of time with unk Shang soaking up some major game. One of the first things he said to me was,

"We didn't want this shit for ya'll."...

"Our plan was to put y'all in college to have ya'll overseeing our family corporations by now."...

"We were gone send some of ya'll to school to be lawyers, financial officers and shit like that."...

"You would have definitely been one of our executive officers."...

"The shit didn't happen that way though!"...

"Look man!"...

"First thing ya gotta know is, that you not gone get rich off this shit!"...

"It's gone give you a damn good head start, but you gotta have a out plan."

We talked daily about a lot of legitimate business ventures. Some other rules he gave me to live by were don't sell to pregnant women or users under the age of eighteen. I was no longer working on the blocks of Wall Street. I took on unk's philosophy which was that the product that we were trading doesn't spoil and there was no need to try to move it all in one day, so it started taking me longer to move product.

I started operating just like every other company in America, opening at a certain time and closing at a certain time every day, ensuring that I came as close to my daily quota as possible. Now that I had set hours of operation my earning potential was limited, only serving a selective group of loyal clientele. Although my daily take home resembled the average weekly work wage, I felt that I was leaving a lot of money on the table.

It didn't take long, but eventually I joined forces with unk Shang. Unk had orchestrated a routine that was very lucrative for the both of us. He established three houses located on the west side of the city to trade out of. There were three women liaisons located at each house that handled all the trade transactions. Those three streams of income were generating massive revenue for us. He told me that it wasn't a good idea for both of us to share the same address and encouraged me to remain at my aunt's house (my mother's youngest sister) which was located on the west side of the city until I finished high school and got my own spot.

We ran a Monday through Friday operation with three daily drop offs, and three daily collections. Every morning before school I would drop off product to each of the houses and collect dough from each of the women. Then on the way home after school I would drop off all the dough that was collected from that morning's collections to unk. I remember pulling up on unk after school the Friday of the first week of the operation. I handed him that morning's collection and he went upstairs with it as he usually did but this time, he called me upstairs shortly after. Unk sent me into the bathroom with two wads of dough to recount for him. He told me the total amount that he had come up with, but he wasn't sure and wanted me to double check it for him. It ended up being like over five hundred dollars more than what unk had originally counted. So, at that very moment I knew then that unk was testing me to see if I was going to do some petty greedy shit and steal from him. I came out of the bathroom and told unk,

"Man I don't know how you counted that but it's over five hundred dollars more than what you told me."

Unk just kind of smiled and looked at me and said,

"Good, cause that's your cut for the week."

That amount was pretty much consistent every Friday for me, that's when unk explained the importance of me keeping a ledger and taught me how to itemize. From that day moving forward I've always kept a ledger even to this very day I do. Me and unk's situation put me in a really good position. Unk bought a Cadillac Humpback Seville, and we would take a ride in it every opportunity that unk was permitted to leave the house during his house arrest. He would always ride me past this abandoned property that looked like it used to be an old ice cream stand. He knew the exact asking price for the property and everything. He was encouraging me to purchase the property, and at the same time reminding me that I needed an out plan, he said,

"You gotta think long-term cause this game we playin right now is short lived!"

Although unk and I had our thing in motion, there were others in the family that were doing their own thing and earning very well.

At this time, unk hands were still somewhat tied so his reach was limited. One evening we were sitting on the porch sipping on a cold Miller High Life, and unk told me that he had a major move on standby that he's been anxious to make. He said,

"Once these people cut me loose, I can start moving like I want to."

While pointing down to the ankle monitor that was on his ankle. Then he went on to start asking me questions pertaining to the law as far as how much prison time different amounts of weight carry. This was before Joe Biden and Clinton's mandatory minimum crime bill was passed into law. Either way, I had no clue and didn't have an answer for unk. The fact that I didn't know and couldn't answer his question frustrated him. I remember unk sitting up on the stair stoop and turning toward me and looking me directly down the barrel of my eyes and saying,

"How the fuck is you in this shit and don't know the mutha-fukin laws!?"...

"Cause if you catch another muthafuckin case nigga, they gone charge ya ass as an adult!"...

"Ain't no more of that juvenile shit ya ass going to the penitentiary!"...

"Ya dig!"...

"The shit is public information you can find in any mutha-fuckin public library!"...

"Everything that offers public access you should be utilizing it!"...

"These muthafuckin laws ain't nothing but weapons they created to use against you!"

"You better learn how to use that same weapon to help you fight back if need be!"...

"Plus, you can avoid a lot of unnecessary shit!"...

"Don't be like all these other simple minded muthafuckas out here!"

He took a quick break to take a swig of his beer and went on to say,

"And all this material shit ain't nothing man!?"...

"The houses, cars and all that shit is nothing!"...

"Ya dig!?"...

"Whatever you get or got now, you can get it again!"...

"Ya understand me!?"

I sat there with him for hours that night while he defined transactions, possessions, and a heap of other shit to me.

I finished my senior year and graduated from high school in 1991. My senior year was an action-packed movie. There were basketball tournaments held every Christmas season, they were known as the "Christmas Tournaments". High schools from all over Michigan would participate in the "Christmas Tournament" the Grand Rapids junior college gymnasium would be at capacity with standing room only. It would be like a fashion show up in there. People would be dressed in their Sunday best. We would come through there deep like superstars rocking all leather NFL jogging suits, Pelle Pelle jackets, leather Eight Ball jackets with the leather pants to match with the jackets, Bally boots and shit like that. I had obtained so much power and influence in high school that I was voted Homecoming king without participating in any school sports or school club activities.

The lifestyle had set me apart from my peers. I was a favorite among the young ladies, they loved young Boonce, although there was a teacher that wasn't receptive to that at all. He attempted to have Big Mac and myself removed from the Homecoming court over some dumb shit, but it wasn't shit he could do about it by that time. There was an influential teacher who took sides with us, besides there was a new era and culture introduced to that high school in 1991 when we changed the game. There were some of us who earned twice that of a teacher's salary that year. Cuban Links, foreign cars and pagers were a part of our uniform. Although I had the Audi, I would drive Solo's truck a lot. He eventually sold it to me, the color had changed to pearl white with an all white leather interior. It was trimmed in gold, sitting on all gold hammers.

During this period of time, I learned Marie was pregnant. I was going to be a father expecting my first son. Bing and Blue were back in Grand Rapids permanently, and my unk Shang had worked his way out of that ankle monitor. Dash was returning from a boot camp program that he was sentenced to for a case he had caught. Solo and Beef both had caught a possession with intent to distribute charges. The Michigan State patrol pulled them over on interstate 96 headed west bound searching the vehicle finding product in a well-hidden compartment. They both were released on bail and immediately lawyered up. Following their release, they were instantly back in action.

We spent a lot of time back and forth on interstate 96 traveling to and from the east and west side of the state. There was one time that I'll never forget. Bing and I had been on the east side of the state for about a few days or so. Raw Dawg had called from the west side of the state to let Solo know he needed more product to trade. So, Bing and I drove with the intention of meeting him halfway in Lansing. We sat there for hours, and Raw Dawg never surfaced. We called Solo only to learn that Raw Dawg car had broken down on the interstate. So, we had to drive back with that same product, which was a considerable amount of weight in our possession. On our way back we decided to travel on highway M-59. There was a police cruiser that we thought was trying to get behind us to make a traffic stop. To me it felt as if they were following us for miles, every traffic light we caught seemed like it lasted for an hour. We both kept our cool, but I just knew that it wouldn't be long before those colorful flashing lights were on our ass pulling us over.

Bingo was still a juvenile, but I would now be charged as an adult on this charge. But thanks be to God almighty that it didn't happen that way, they never got directly behind us, the police cruiser didn't pull us over that night. We made it back and as we were pulling into the driveway, I thought to myself

"If my unk Shang knew I had made a move like this he would've blown a fuse."

I remember telling myself after catching that first case as a juvenile that I would never put myself in that type of compromising situation again, but there I was.

It wasn't long after my graduation that things changed dramatically for all of us. This all happened when our supplier changed. Unk's reach and relationships have always stretched across the country and beyond. He finally made that move that he had been anxiously waiting to make. He established a situation that changed the entire landscape for all of us. His influence and connections opened a flood gate of product, and the purchase price dropped tremendously; we made a huge purchase, Solo being a majority shareholder. We have never been a gang; we were always self-made men. The after-trade profit margin was way over fifty percent.

At this point all of us began wholesale trading, except for Raw Dawg he was moving a little differently. He was cooking the product by the buckets, manufacturing hammers (large pieces) and the traders that worked the blocks of Wall Street worshiped him. Most of your favorite and well-known traders in multiple cities (whether they were directly on the blocks of Wall Street or the executives of those blocks) were either directly or indirectly trading our product. Unk Shang told me to never deal with no more than three or four people directly in any given city. I held on to that advice the entire time. There isn't but a handful of individuals in my hometown that can say they've done a face-to-face transaction with me, with a few of them being deceased (God bless their souls), which would include Spade, Big Ike, Marble, and Big Mac's nephew Fig. Everything was working like clockwork. The earnings began to increase and so did my ego.

Never have I been in possession of that amount of cash belonging solely to me. With that amount of currency at my disposal, I was ready to buy cars, jewelry and all the shiny shit that is associated with that lifestyle, but unk would always preach against attracting any attention to what we had going on. He was so against it that he would become irate and infuriated whenever he talked about the reasons that I shouldn't be purchasing so many extravagant items. He would say things like,

"What the fuck would you go and buy that for man!?"...

"I'm a foreman on my job and cain't justify buying that kinda shit!"

The more cash I accumulated the less I took heed to unk's advice. Slowly but surely, I started to fade from unk's tutelage, and began maneuvering how I saw fit. Obviously, it caused a clash between us and put a damper on our relationship. Not just my relationship but many of our relationships with unk went sour. My humble opinion, I think we got beside ourselves when we scrapped unk's blueprint for the family's future. Just like the scene from the movie "Baby Boy" unk was teaching me about guns and butter, but at that age I couldn't comprehend why I couldn't have both. Although I continued to follow much of the game that unk had sprinkled on me, keeping a low profile wasn't one of them. Bottom line, I got too big for my britches. But if I knew what I knew today I would have stayed under unk's deodorant (his wing).

Marie had given birth to a healthy baby boy; my son had made his way to the earth. With every intention of giving him everything that I didn't have I started neglecting the most import-ant thing, my time. Marie and our son were comfortably situated in a luxury apartment out of the way. My little sister lived there with us as well. I learned of the flat through DQ. He and his lady friend were already there residing in a suite. Solo eventually occupied a suite there also with his lady friend. After my little sister moved in with us, I enrolled her into middle school.

When we arrived at her orientation a crowd of students were staring in awe at the car as we pulled into the parking lot. She got out of the car with a Salt-N-Pepa asymmetrical haircut wear-ing pants that were leather on the front and jean on the back. Her rider boots were matching with the leather portion of her pants. She was a big deal among her peers. Her father claimed that I was ruining her. One day he said to me,

"You're the reason she acts the way she do."...

"You done spoiled that girl!"

Ever since my little sister was born, I've been responsible for her as if she was my first child. My son wasn't wanting for anything worldly either, but I was never present. In and out of state regularly traveling the interstates, I wasn't spending any real time with my toddler son. An oath was made between me and myself when I was a kid, that I would be present in my children's life. I must confess that the first few years of my first-born son's life I wasn't honoring that oath, although I justified it quite a bit. The volume of cash I began having in my possession started to alter my mentality in more ways than one. It reminds me of when my unk Shang used to say,

"The dealer becomes just as much of an addict as the user."

To accrue substantial amounts of cash in such an expeditious manner, that releases large amounts of dopamine into your bloodstream. The higher the stakes, the more of it's released. Having too much of that shit causes you to be aggressive and have trouble controlling your impulses. Even though Scarface is only a character from a movie, you witness as his empire grows the amount of dopamine released into his bloodstream increases causing his character to morph into something totally different from when he originally started. Even if he hadn't started using his own product, nine times out of ten the results would have been the same. We tend to become consumed with the chase, the money, and the power, never realizing we are intoxicated. I was in that position at an age when I wasn't even legally old enough to buy alcoholic beverages. Even though I've seen and have been around large sums of cash a great deal of my life, it was different being so young in control of the utilization of such an enormous amount of revenue. My ledger could be compared to one of a small grocery chain.

The individual I had become started causing Marie a considerable amount of turmoil. I have always had the utmost respect for her, never putting anything directly in her face, but the streets were talking. I was going against the game as I knew it. I began letting my dick beat my hand out. In other words, I started granting women access to me, allowing them to be entertained and participate in having the experience of being with me free of charge, in exchange for some pussy.

Let's be clear, none of them were ever gifted with cash money, but I did permit them to take part in my lifestyle. That was a no-no where I'm from, if they were not bringing any money or something back to contribute to what I was building, their access would have been denied if I were following the rules of the game as I knew it. A woman must put some money in your hands before you can know if she really likes you or not. Because the goal was to reach beyond any of her physical pleasures. You didn't want to be her best sexual partner, you wanted to be her favorite man. That's how the game was served to me. In my heart of hearts, I knew that the time that I was donating to them at no cost, was the time that Marie and my son deserved. But at that period, I had lost sight of some critical aspects of the game, including my out plan.

It was one of those days that my grandmother (my father's mother) sent word that she wanted to see me. She would always send word through my mother, my other grandmother, or one of my mother's sisters. It was really a code for her and I, I knew what it was concerning. When I made it to my grandmother's house (my father's mother) I realized that Ski was there, he was living with our grandmother at the time. After sitting there visiting with her for a minute handling the business that we had to take care of I got up to head out of the door then Ski got up to follow behind me. When we made it outside, he said that he needed to holler at me about something. As I was opening my car door to get in, Ski opened the passenger door to get into the car with me. We exchanged a few words like we usually do then he said to me,

"Man, we should start a record label and put out a CD.".

"It's a company called Disc Makers that'll make'em for five dollars and we can sell'em for ten dollars."

I put the key into the ignition and started the car, turned to Ski looking him directly in his eyes and said,

"Man I ain't no muthafuckin rapper, you see this shit I'm doin?".

"I'm doin this shit til I die, I'm gone have a muthafucka bringing me my newspaper!"

At the time, the Dayton Family was a popular group on the streets in our region, and although Ski presented an excellent idea and game plan at the time, I completely stopped watering the seed that unk had planted. A few days later I paid a visit to my other grandmother (my mother's mother). We sat there and talked for a minute when she asked if I didn't mind taking her to the grocery store. I obliged; we never refused her request. She instructed me to collect her shoes and purse as she began brushing her hair. I inserted her feet into the orthopedic shoes firmly tying the laces, and she retrieved a scarf from her purse to cover her head. We made our way out the door as I was assisting her down the stairs of the porch she stopped to look up and said,

"Ooh Wee that's a pretty car!"

Then she cleared the next step making her way to the car. After we settled in the car and began driving for a minute, Granny looked at me and said "Only rich men drive these kinda cars. Boy ya tellin the people what ya doin. Now ya know when they talk about, ya'll, I always say I rather see my boys sellin it than using it, but ya gotta do somethin else. Then she stated,

"It seem to me ya gotta enough now to do something else."

I started telling her what I thought she wanted to hear, that I had a plan put together for going back to finish college, then starting a business. She said,

"Boy yo ass gone wish ya was under my bed eating cat shit with a broom straw by the time ya get done doin what ya doin!"

She wasn't lying.

It was another rotation around the sun and another summer was on deck. Our territories had increased even more along with our earnings. We all had purchased exotic vehicles and had them customized with white lambskin leather interior with gigantic custom body kits. Solo had his car customized with a wide body Testarossa kit with the offset tires, and we stopped traffic in every city we drove through. The Cincinnati Kool Jazz Festival was on the calendar that year for us, and we arrived in extraordinary fashion. There were all types of fly ass cars at the festival that summer, however, we stood out from the crowd when we pulled into the hotel entrance.

The gigantic custom body kits and the all-white butter soft leather interior in that many cars in a row, may have been the reason. I believe we were like six or seven vehicles deep and unk "H" was leading the procession in the big body S550 Mercedes Benz sitting on chrome Hammers, with the gold Mercedes centerpiece emblem in them. The hotel valet didn't even park our vehicles, they left them all out front parked outside the hotel entrance. Young ladies were walking up to us asking to take a picture with us and our cars. We were attracting more attention than some of the celebrities that were staying at the same hotel that we were in. Our suites were on the same floor as many of them, without doing any name dropping. There were a few of your favorites. It was another action-packed weekend, one of many to remember.

Raw Dawg didn't make the trip, he decided to stay home to attend to his day-to-day operations. Upon our arrival back in the city we were informed that Raw Dawg had been arrested and taken into custody charged with possession with intent to distribute. The bail amount was paid, and Raw Dawg was released on bond, back to business as usual while preparing to fight the new case. Raw Dawg was much like our unk Shang when it came to keeping a low profile. That led me to believe that his arrest was related to a catch and release informant (an individual caught in the act of a crime and released back to the streets to cooperate with law enforcement). Raw Dawg never bought an exotic car or any flashy items to draw attention to himself; he always flew under the radar.

The vehicle he drove was a pickup truck and he utilized that for the moving company that he owned. He was working on a project; it was a Grand Prix that had like sixty-five hundred dollars' worth of car stereo equipment in it. Him and Dash were the first people that I knew with remote controls to their car sound systems. Other than that, he carried himself like he didn't have a dime to his name. So, if you didn't know Raw Dawg, you would have never known that he was generating the excessive amounts of revenue that he was. He liked to do a lot of fishing and different types of activities; one included cooking for the entire Oakdale neighborhood.

Raw Dawg would buy large amounts of meat to put on the grill, fill multiple coolers with beers, prepare huge pots of side dishes like spaghetti and potato salad. His process would begin early in the morning so by the afternoon when we would all be stopping by our grandmother's house just to check in, it would end up being a full day of fellowship for us. We would do a store run to buy more bags of ice and cases of beer for the coolers, so many cases that there would be cases left over for the next day. People from the neighborhood would stop and congregate for hours; they would be coming and going all day. Pretty customized cars would line the curbs for blocks on each side of the street. Young ladies from different neighborhoods would ride by blowing their car horns all day, there were some of the young ladies that would stop their cars in the middle of the street holding up traffic yelling out random different names. They were encouraged to pull over and park to come fellowship with us for a while, a lot of them did. Big Dirty would always have a crowd around him watching as he demonstrated different boxing techniques and fighting strategies, while making sound effects of his punches,

"Bink, Bink, Bomp!"

Those would be the type of sounds you would hear him make while he was shadow boxing. The fellowship would last from the afternoon until late at night, typically on a Friday or Saturday. Many of us would leave from Oakdale and head directly to the nightclub. We were always closing the nightclub down. Parker's burger joint would be the next stop afterwards. You couldn't end your night without getting a few of those famous burgers. There would be a waiting line a block long with people eager to purchase a few. Those types of nights occurred often whenever we were in Grand Rapids.

It was one Saturday that DQ hosted a birthday party for his woman at a local venue in Grand Rapids. Pretty much everyone was in attendance that night. After the party was over Bingo and Big Dirty were on Oakdale when they noticed some unfamiliar faces standing near our grandmother's house. As they approached the gentlemen to address them gunshots rang out echoing across the west end of Oakdale. They both suffered multiple gunshot wounds to their abdomen and lower body. Big Dirty and Bing both survived the shooting but were in the hospital in critical condition for months. Unk "H" and everyone was furious and the fact that there was no target to revenge frustrated unk "H" even more. He made sure that he did a thorough investigation, unk went over everything with a fine-tooth comb looking for any details. Integrating any and everybody he thought could give him a lead.

After months of being in the hospital Bing and Big Dirty were eventually discharged, both wearing colostomy bags. They had to utilize wheelchairs as well for a time. The shooting left them both in an unpleasant condition. Seeing them in that shape hurt me to the inner parts of my stomach. There were never any leads to help identify and locate the gunmen. It took some time, but they licked their wounds as Big Dirty would describe it, ultimately healing and making complete recoveries.

All these events were taking place around the time I reconciled with my father. We hadn't spoken to each other for like a year or better. One day Marie and I stopped by my grandmother's house (his mother), and he happened to be there. As we entered the dining room, I saw him sitting at the kitchen table with my aunt and uncle. I proceeded to enter the kitchen to greet my aunt and uncle and before I could open my mouth you heard my father say,

"Player! Player!"

Which kind of caught me off guard. But truth be told, my heart was relieved to be reconciled with my father, we may not have seen eye to eye all the time, but I loved that man. From that day forward my father and I relationship grew beyond father and son, and we became like brothers. Milwaukee soon became his permanent residence for some time, he eventually moved out to the west coast. But when he relocated to Milwaukee, he had gotten remarried to a black woman named "Marcy" who was beautiful inside and out. From day one she embraced me as her very own. She was a stockbroker at Milwaukee's top brokerage firm. Just outright sharp, always dressed to the tee in executive attire, her hair fell past her shoulders; she was upper echelon, a true class act. But don't let the smooth taste fool you, because she was game as they come. Together they became a force to be reckoned with, my father would always say,

"Don't try this at home!"

Whenever you would see the two of them together.

My father and I began hanging like shoes on a power line. I was visiting him and his wife in Milwaukee on a regular basis. It became a second home for me. I even had a small wardrobe there that I kept for a change of clothes. On one visit he and I were shooting pool in their basement, and he was pretty much giving me the same game my unk Shang had been giving me, but he and I had never talked about the business like that. Typically, he would discuss the pimp game with me. He said,

"Player."...

"I remember before I went to the joint."...

"We was gettin money like forty going north!"...

"One time, me and ya uncle "H" was over ya aunts house (DQ, Red Man and Big Dirty mother) and she told us that our run would come to a end one day."...

"She was lettin us know, we better start thinkin bout what we can do with all the paper we had."...

"But shit was so good for us, I start believin that the shit would never end."...

"Ya aunt was tryin to give us that real game!"

What was so crazy about the conversation, is my aunt had just given me the same game not long before he was serving it to me. He went on to say,

"See man, if you can walk away, you can get away!"...

"Ya gotta be the sharpest pencil in the pencil sharpener player"

Today I understood that my father wasn't really upset with me, but worried. He was concerned about my well-being; he never wanted me to have to walk that same yard that he did.

Senator Joe Biden had been working diligently to have legislation passed and President Bill Clinton signed into law what would be known as the Crime Bill. This new "tough on crime" legislation mandated a minimum sentence of five-years without parole for individuals convicted of trafficking five grams of crack (not even a quarter of an ounce), ten-year minimum sentence without parole for individuals convicted of trafficking 50 grams of crack (just over an ounce and a half), individuals convicted of possessing crack cocaine would receive the same sentence as someone who possessed a hundred times more powder cocaine (coke). A person could receive up to life in prison depending on the number of grams they were in possession of.

These harsh convictions and football number sentences created a new era and a record number of snitches that gave the game a black eye, mass incarceration of black and brown people across America. I don't believe the ink was dry on the new bill at the time that Raw Dawg caught his second case. There was no doubt in my mind that he was hand delivered by a cooperating informant. The Vice Unit knew exactly what they were looking for and where to look. They would never have figured it out on their own, it would have had to be someone that he had allowed to come behind the curtains to do business with him. With the amount of clientele that Raw Dawg was servicing it made a long list of people that were suspect. Law enforcement offered him the alternative option of cooperating, and he had more than enough to barter with. He could have served every one of us on a silver platter, but Raw Dawg kept his mouth closed and took the lengthy sentence on the chin.

He was eventually convicted of possession with intent to distribute and given a ten-to-twenty-year mandatory minimum sentence for not cooperating with law enforcement. Which meant that he had to serve a mandatory ten-year minimum sentence without parole. I remember going to visit with him in the penitentiary, and that low-spirited feeling that I had during my trip from

Muskegon back to Grand Rapids. Leaving the correctional facility without Raw Dawg never sat right with me. We kept our lines of communication open by writing letters as well. He would always end all his letters with,

"It's not that we plan to fail, but we fail to plan."

Our letters never contained any information pertaining to the business, that would only be discussed during our personal visits. The first visit I remember him telling me basically that despite how anyone wants to glamorize, or make it some type of badge of honor, the penitentiary is no place to be proud of. He repeated to me what an OG had shared with him, the OG said,

"Two or three years of leisure ain't worth two or three decades of hell."...

"Look here, a steady drip gone beat a flood or drought any day."

We all would visit Raw Dawg frequently; I would bring my son with me on many of those visits. Raw Dawg would be escorted to the visiting area wearing Coogi sweaters, Pelle Pelle leather jackets and all types of designer wear. We purchased every food selection displayed in the vending machines (minus the pork products). During the warmer months we would sit in the picnic area and watch my son while he enjoyed himself on the playground equipment. Me and Raw Dawg would break bread and fellowship bringing him up to speed with what was happening in the outside world. Red Man acquired Raw Dawg's clientele and territory. After Red Man vetted Raw Dawg's downline, he eventually broke ties with more than half of them. This allowed Raw Dawg to maintain a portion of the market share while he was away.

Business was good, the two of my clients that had bulk goods on consignment were paying on their due dates. The other two of my clients were purchasing their own re-up along with paying their consignment tab consistently. I initially only had three individuals in my downline that I was doing business with directly in my hometown. Big Mac's nephew Fig became my fourth. Starting out we never conducted a face-to-face transaction. Our business relationship began with a long-time friend of mine named Flossy, who happened to be Fig's cousin (his father was Flossy's uncle).

My family and Flossy's family had a history dating back to the 70's which made us family. Fig's father (Flossy's uncle) and my father had been friends since adolescence. Flossy approached me one day concerning some business. He let me know that he wasn't looking for consignment, he was fronting his own bill. The amount of weight that he was attempting to purchase caught my interest, making me reconsider opening my books and taking on another client in my hometown. Flossy made the first two purchases before I ran into Fig at Northland Mall on the east side of the state, both of us carrying two handfuls of shopping bags. We gave each other some dap, then had a brief conversation telling each other what we had just purchased out of the stores. That's when Fig said,

"That's not Flossy buying that from you, that's me."

This is when I learned that Flossy was operating in the capacity of a liaison (middleman). From that day forward Fig began doing business directly with me, and believe me when I say,

"We did a whole lot of it!"

I always liked and respected the way that he conducted his business, like me he was advanced for his age. Big Ike and Marble were my first two recruits when I began my new business venture in wholesaling. Their invoices were paid punctually, never being a dollar short. Re-ups were on a weekly schedule, their dedication and commitment to the business was proven by the steady increase of their weekly sales turnover. They were relentless on the blocks of Wall Street; they were top level executives trading any amount of weight that they were supplied with. Spade was an OG, and he conducted business like one. From the way that he would have his money organized to the terminology that he used. Some of these individuals were responsible for supplying product to many others who had no idea that they were part of my network and the downline of independent distributors.

One evening I was cruising through the city, and I stopped for a red light at the corner of Eastern and Franklin, Marble pulled next to me. We both rolled down our windows, he asked me if I could pull over so that he could holler at me. If you've ever watched the movie Paid-In-Full, Franklin Street was the stage like the scene in front of Willie's Burgers, times ten. Fly cars would be bumper to bumper for at least six blocks, with side huddles gathered on the off streets. Everybody that was somebody would bring their cars out to parade them through. Marble followed me into the bank parking lot that was located on the corner. He was approaching my car as I was getting out. As he came closer, I noticed that the front of his shirt was bulging resembling that of a beer belly. The first thing he said was,

"Boonce I know this ain't how ya do shit, but can I give you this bread I owe you?"

He began to reach under his shirt to show me, I placed my hand on top of his to stop him from revealing the bag. My driver's side door was still open, so I told him to have a seat in my car and just put it on the floor. He then stressed to me how relieved he was that we had crossed paths, and explained the reason that it was so urgent that he had to give it to me at that time. Now I have a bag of cash on the floor of the car that I didn't want to ride around with.

Just so happens I see Ski coming out of the corner store, I beep the horn and swoop down on him. I asked him what he was getting into, he told me that he had just stopped to grab a couple of beers on his way home. After I confirmed that he was going directly home I reached for the bag of cash under my legs and asked him if he would take the bag home with him and hold on to it. Weeks went by before I made it over there to retrieve the bag from Ski and there was not one dime missing. He was always one that I could trust not to steal from me.

The term indictment became very popular among the culture during that era. Keeping your head on a swivel moving with extreme caution and strategically was mandatory. The game was changing by the day. Unk Shang was set up by a gentleman whom he had history with; they had done some major business in the past. Although it was back in the 70's when the two had last conducted any business together. The gentleman had done a long stretch in the penitentiary having a well-established reputation of being a stand-up guy since back in the day. Unfortunately for my unk Shang the gentleman was no longer living up to that reputation. He assisted law enforcement with catching unk red handed, which would have been impossible without his cooperation.

Unk was charged and convicted of possession with intent to distribute and given a thirty-five-to-sixty five-year mandatory minimum sentence as a habitual criminal. Although me and unk hadn't been on the best of terms since our disagreement, I was crushed by the news. I went to visit him in the penitentiary, the first chance that I got. Unk was escorted to the visiting area as the secured door was opening, he stepped through the doorway wearing a HBCU themed sweatshirt. His large body frame stood there as he scanned the room. Once he caught sight of me, he smiled and began walking in my direction. He embraced me with the type of hug that a father would give to a prodigal son. There was no mention of our past disagreements, we picked up where we left off. I shared with him a few plans that I had under my sleeves, and he said to me,

"Me and you gone be trading places!"...

"I'm working on an appeal to get out of here, and you working on getting in here."...

"Shit ain't the same out there no more man, you don't know who you are dealing with today!"...

"And I know ya tight wad ass gotta enough money saved to start you a new life somewhere!"

Looking at me with a serious smile. Then he said,

"This muthafuckin penitentiary ain't no place for players like us man!"

That's when unk started sharing the details of all the events that led up to his arrest. It was a lot involved with his case including information concerning his nephews. The Feds approached him offering a deal that would land him a ten-year sentence in exchange for us. But because unk didn't take the bait somehow the Feds granted the state of Michigan jurisdiction of his case. Leaving that visiting room, unk gave me a lot to think about.

It was back to business as usual when I received the news that one of my clients by the name of Spade had been arrested and charged with possession. All I could think about at that moment was that it was all over for me. So, I laid low for a few days before I received a page from Spade. I was hesitant to call him back, but I wanted to feel him out to see how I was going to maneuver moving forward. Not to mention he owed a large sum of money for what he had been given on consignment. Calling him back was risky but I reached out anyway, and he was explaining to me how his greed got him jammed up. He told me that he had dealt with someone, and that he shouldn't have, going on to tell me that he still had product and a substantial amount of his outstanding bill.

Before hanging up the phone I instructed him to just hold on to it until he was able to pay the remaining balance. Not even two days later did I receive a page from him letting me know that he was prepared to pay his debt in full. Our meeting location would always be in high traffic areas. I met with all my clients at these types of locations. Only a couple of them ever received product from me in a hand-to-hand transaction. My routine was arriving at the location twenty minutes earlier than the time that I would give them to meet. I would place the product in a location that was far away from me, sometimes disguising it as trash in multiple fast-food bags.

This time I chose Meijer Thrifty Acres as our meeting location. Arriving there oversuspicious with no product I parked my car at the opposite end of the parking lot. As I walked through the parking lot, I studied my surroundings and for some damn reason I was looking for the van like you see in the movies. Went into the store to buy something and at the time that I was walking out I recognized his car in our agreed meeting location. With an extreme uneasiness of mind, I approached his vehicle and got inside. Remember that he told me it was greed that got him jammed up, and it was greed that told me to get in the car. His outstanding balance was a great deal of money, making it tough for me to walk away from it. The rationale behind my decision was that there was no product to exchange for the money. He handed over a Sibley's Shoes shopping bag with the money in it and started briefing me on his legal situation. My words were far and few between. I listened to him very closely paying attention to the details. After he explained everything, I told him that I would be in touch with him and he replied,

"I'm good man, I'm done!"...

"I gotta few dollars put up."...

I'm gone get ready to go do this time they give me."...

"I know you gotta lot of bread already."...

"Shit, to be honest you gotta enough bread in that bag I just gave you."...

"Boonce they ain't gone let us get it all man!"

There was a feeling of relief once he spoke those words, it was confirmation to me that Spade was thorough. To this day I have the utmost respect for him. He's a real stand-up guy.

Back to having only three clients in my hometown and a notion to walk away from it all. I stopped by my grandmother's house on Oakdale, when I walked in the door my grandmother was in the dining room sitting on the edge of her medical bed. She allowed me to make it into the dining room before she said,

"Ya uncle called earlier and wanted me to let ya know that the Snowman is dead."

Snowman was our supplier, he had been gunned down in cold blood outside of his oceanfront estate. We hadn't long ago made it back from visiting with him, we stayed for a little over a week. Snowman always showed us great hospitality on our business trips. He would give us the keys to his cars and everything, I mean really roll out the red carpet for us.

First King was a strip club in California that he would take us to. I don't knock the hustle of a stripper, however I never had an interest in strip clubs. The concept of strip clubs seemed to be against my nature. It was too much like tricking to me. But the way that Snowman had it arranged for us made it a different type of party. I witnessed some crazy shit in that establishment. There was a soul food restaurant named Dulan's in Inglewood, CA that he turned us on to. It seems to me that I recall it being owned and operated by the Muslim brothers at the time. It was some of the best soul food you could eat. We made sure that we would go there whenever we took business trips.

Our visits became so frequent that we started crossing paths with actors, actresses and west coast rappers on a regular basis. There are a lot of comedians that I remember seeing early in their career at The Comedy Store, that are now household names today. Snowman gave me the nickname "No Bet" because the first time we ever visited him for a face to face sit down, they all ended up shooting dice betting large sums of money. I'm not a gambler never have been due to the game unk Shang had served me, he told me,

"Don't fuck with gamblin, it's just another bad habit."

When Snowman realized that I wasn't participating in the dice game he looked at me and said,

"Bet ya brother don't pass!"

My reply was,

"No bet!"

He repeated that for like two more rolls, each time I replied with the same response. From that night on he referred to me as "No Bet". The passing of Snowman raised concerns about our future business endeavors, but unk's influence and connections put us in contact with a new supplier. I never laid eyes on the new supplier or had any interaction with him. Red Man handled a lot of the politics and face-to-face meetings with him. But things were never the same for us after Snowman's death. A few of the loads following his death were pure garbage. That never happened on Snowman's watch.

We all brought in the new year in Milwaukee together. It was another one of those classic nights to remember, it probably was the last night that we all celebrated together in that capacity. We attended a party at a popular night-club in Milwaukee. From wall to wall the establishment was filled with players and play-ettes. There were mink coats, mink hats, alligator, crocodile and snakeskin at every turn of the head. The DJ publicly endorsed us over the PA system all throughout the night, we purchased so much Dom Pérignon, that the club supply ran out.

There was an owner of a liquor store at the party that night. Unk "H" sent him to open his store to bring us back more cases of Dom Pérignon. I don't remember what time it was, but I do remember that the city businesses were closed. If you've ever been to Milwaukee, then you know that liquor stores close at nine pm. The owner of the nightclub was in no position to take issue with unk bringing outside liquor into his establishment, since he was in unk's pocket. While we were waiting for the Dom Pérignon to arrive, someone at the party sent bottles of Moët & Chandon over to our tables. The moment that I recognized that it was Moët & Chandon sent over I said,

"Who sent this ole cheap ass fifty dollar a bottle shit over here!?"

Unk "H" and all my people started laughing hysterically, we still laugh about that to this very day. Driving back to Grand Rapids the following night I experienced a nasty car accident on Interstate Highway 94 East. In the process of attempting to pass a semi-truck, the truck slightly veered off into my lane nicking the front end of the car causing the car to skid across the icy road. After smacking a bridge barrier, a couple of times, the car came to a rest. The wind had been knocked out of me and I couldn't catch my breath, when I did catch my breath, it had become extremely painful to breathe. Soon an ambulance arrived taking me to a hospital in St. Joseph, MI. The doctors performed an x-ray examination and the results showed that the only injuries I suffered were some bruised ribs. I escaped the terrible accident with minor injuries. Someone was there at the hospital to pick me up after I was discharged that following morning. Apart from the accident, and a few bruised ribs, the year got off to a good start and the business was moving with precision.

The new year brought on new clients as well. I began playing the role of liaison with a couple of Solo clients who lived in my hometown. Solo started to avoid visiting Grand Rapids all

together. "Great" was one of Solo clients whose method of con-
ducting business I've always admired. He was born and raised in
my neighborhood, a high-ranking executive on the blocks of Wall
Street. He was another individual that could handle any amount
of weight, he'd move product like Amazon. Despite the fact revenue was surging, I made the decision that I was going to leave
the business. I informed my family who were involved in the business and all my clients across the board that my time was drawing
near. They were all aware that I was going out of business once
I depleted the last of my supply. I began the liquidation process,
bringing my business to an end. I sold all my cars including the
customized exotic one, and in turn purchased one car, a Cadillac
DeVille. The focus now was on collecting all outstanding debts,
selling all my inventory, and raising as much capital as possible.
My father once told me "If you can walk away, you can get away."
I was walking away at the peak of my business. No one really
believed me; they thought that I was just switching gears trans-
forming to a lower profile.

As I began washing my hands of the business my grandmother informed me that two detectives stopped by her house
asking about me. I started thinking intensely about my most recent
transactions, and what it could possibly be pertaining to. They
had to have been watching my grandmother's house, because
not even half an hour after being there an unmarked police car
drove up. Two white men exited the vehicle greeting me by my
government name, followed by the mispronunciation of my nickname. In the back of my mind, I instantly started thinking shit like
indictment or one of my clients had given me up. Then the men
introduced themselves as officers of the Grand Rapids Police
Department Detective Unit.

They went on to tell me that my name had been mentioned
in the connection to a kidnapping and torture case, by the victim.
The victim made known to the authorities that he had supposedly
stolen a considerable amount of product from one of my family
members. He allegedly claimed that he and I were together at the
time that he was taken against his will and placed in a car trunk
with his hands and feet tied. The victim claimed that he was driven

to a secluded location where he remained tied up and three men severely disciplined him. He reported that he escaped by managing to get his hands unfastened after being left unattended for a long period. I explained to the detectives that I had been out of town and had no knowledge of the incident. They assured me that at the conclusion of their investigation if the evidence proved different that they would be back.

"If we do have to come back, it will not be for further questioning."...

"It'll be to put you in handcuffs."

One of the detectives said as they both began walking back to the unmarked car.

Semi-retired with one foot in and one foot out, I asked Marie for her hand in marriage, to move out of the state with her and my son to start over. She said yes, our wedding was a classic event, Shaft was my Best Man. It turned out to basically be a citywide high school reunion for classes from the late 60's through the early 90's. Top OG players and playettes, block of Wall Street executives, corporate executives, School Superintendents, city officials, County Commissioners and this list goes on. One of those "You had to be there" moments.

I originally had my sights set on moving to Tacoma, Washington after the wedding, but we decided to move to Milwaukee so that she could visit her family in Michigan more often. However, Milwaukee was short lived, the "lifestyle" was still reeking from my pores. So, I decided that it was best to move Marie and my son back to Grand Rapids so that she would have easier access to her family while I tightened up the loose ends. After some time, I was out of stock and had traded the last of my supply. That was it, I was officially out of business. With a topped off thirty gallon Hefty garbage bag, and two pillowcases full of capital in the trunk of my Cadillac Deville, I had no plan. Plenty enough to start a new life with my son and newlywed wife, but I fumbled that opportunity. I could have easily started any business that I desired or just simply found employment and sat my ass down somewhere.

A year or so passed and I had not done any business generating any revenue. Still frequently visiting Milwaukee for weeks
on end my capital began to run low. It all reverts to the game unk
Shang had served me, and the saying Raw Dawg would end all his
letters with "It's not that we plan to fail, we fail to plan." During my
oasis there were always former clients and prospects who were
campaigning to become potential clients, reaching out and sending word about doing some business. As I've mentioned no one
outside of family members believed that I was out of business. My
connections were still active, and the temptation grew stronger
as my capital grew weaker. I eventually justified it by convincing
myself that if I played the role of a liaison brokering the deals, I
wasn't "technically" in business.

I began brokering deals earning a very generous commis-
sion. After a few transactions I ended up purchasing myself a new
Mercedes Benz, I bought it off my unk "H". I tried to deny it at the
time, but I was addicted to the lifestyle. What I learned was that

walking away from the business was easier said than done. Unk Shang's influence opened another door for us from the penitentiary. He had made the acquaintance of a Vato who had hands on the outside world. It was a different product and a different market; his people were manufacturers and suppliers of herbs. Unk "H" made the connection with the people on the outside, they spoke very little English. At their first meeting they supplied unk with a massive amount of herbs, all on consignment. That's the kind of weight my unk Shang's name carried. Unk "H" gave me so much of that shit that I didn't know where to store it right away. I spread it out, keeping it in different locations. Now I had shares in a new market, and brokering multiple deals in another.

My new position as liaison was working out splendidly, but not long after starting my new venture a bombshell was dropped on me, I had gotten word that my unk Shang had taken ill in the penitentiary, he was diagnosed with cancer, and it got the better of him. Unk "H", my grandmother, my aunt (my mother's youngest sister) and I all went to visit him. The correctional facility would only allow us to go see him one at a time due to him being housed in the infirmary-level care hospice unit. I was the last one to go in and visit with him. The correction officer escorted me back to the unit, I didn't know what to expect or what to be prepared for. The walk getting there was an experience within itself. It seemed the further we walked the tighter the hallway appeared to be as if the walls on both sides were closing in. My heart was pounding with an anxious and nervous feeling in my stomach.

The minute I stepped into the doorway I saw unk resting in the hospital bed. He heard us entering the room then turned to look to see who it was. When he recognized that it was me his frail frame lifted from the hospital bed sitting straight up. In a weak raspy voice, he said,

"Uncle Bunts!"

We gave one another some dap then embraced with a hug. I felt some strength in the grip of his handshake, but his body felt fragile as I pulled him to the front part of my chest. After we let go of our embrace, we looked at each other eye to eye, I began to choke up, becoming unable to speak, unk told me,

"Be strong! Let God do his thing!"

Collecting myself, I took a seat in the chair that was located next to the bed. Like any other time, unk didn't hesitate to initiate the discussion. It was a heavy conversation, unk shared some of his final thoughts with me. I found myself in an advanced honors class soaking up some major game. He laid some shit on me that day that I'll take to the grave, it'll be buried with me. The visit had drawn to its close, so we concluded exactly how we kicked it off. Our embrace and handshake locked; we held each other longer than usual. It would be our last and final embrace. The last words that I heard him say were,

"Take care of ya business!"

Believe me, that wasn't just a cliche for him. Whenever you heard unk say,

"Take care of ya business"

He meant just that. To this day I stand on his last words. Two or three days later following our visit, the correctional facility contacted a member of our family to inform us that my unk Shang had given up the ghost. He died in the penitentiary.

My wife, my son, and my newborn daughter plus myself were all at my mother's house visiting. I met up with my wife over there, we had driven different vehicles. At this time my little sister who was pregnant with my nephew was now living with our mother. My sister had just finished cooking tacos when my pager started vibrating. I recognized the number right away; it was a client that I was in the process of brokering a deal with. I was expecting to hear from them, so I called the number back right away to set a time and meeting location. All the purchasing agreements remained the same. My wife said she'd wait there with the kids until I returned. By the time that I made it back I realized that my wife was gone, her car was no longer parked outside. As I was getting out of my car, I noticed my sister coming out of the front door with a distraught expression on her face and tears accumulating in her eyes. In an unsteady voice she explained to me that the Grand Rapids Police Department had raided our mother's house while I was gone. She told me that they had burst through the door screaming,

"Grand Rapids Police Department! Search warrant! Get on the ground!"

My wife, my newborn daughter, and my sister were in the house. My son was playing on the porch when the police arrived. He was put on the ground for a short period before being placed into the back of a police cruiser. They held him there until the search was complete. My wife and sister were handcuffed and placed on the couch while they conducted their search. Members of the task force eventually placed my newborn daughter into my wife's lap, handcuffing her hands in front so that she would be able to hold the baby. The search was finished, they came up empty handed, because there was nothing to find to begin with. A task force officer did mention a family member whose name was specifically listed on the search warrant.

Never had that side of the business affected uninvolved family members. My mind began racing, I wasn't sure if the client whose deal I had just brokered was connected with it or not. However, I never orchestrated another deal for them again. They paged me a couple of times the following week, but on no account did I return the call. My intuition was telling me that it was time to walk away for good. I came up with a set goal amount to accumulate and the number of deals that I would need to broker to reach that goal. Once that amount was achieved, I was leaving the business permanently. Moving forward I became even more selective of who I chose to broker deals for, mainly former clients of mine and a couple of individuals that had been affiliated with us in the past. At this time my connection was no longer interested in the Grand Rapids market, so there were no more deliveries being made. Some of the clients did not want to travel to complete their transactions, they preferred to continue to conduct business locally. I didn't want to lose any revenue, so I decided to add to the risk of the penitentiary chances that I was already taking.

Now I've involved myself in the logistics of transporting the product to a handful of Grand Rapids clients. There was a hefty traveling expense taxed on the selling price, but those clients had no issue with paying it. Amtrak and the Greyhound Lines were being utilized frequently to complete many of the transactions. I would only travel on the days that there were professional sporting events being held in the appointed hand-off city. A ticket to the event would be purchased whether I attended the venue or not. I would wear the home or visiting team's athletic apparel along with other team paraphernalia. It gave me the appearance of a die-hard fan, planned for an overnight or two-day trip. A few of the clients would meet me in the hand-off city and I would return with the other client's product. The system was consistent, and it was getting me that much closer to my goal.

Then it all took a left turn, and the train jumped the track. I ended up brokering a few deals that involved some bad business practices, and longtime clients had taken humongous losses associated with those deals. Many of them were expecting some type of compensation, and rightfully so. Unfortunately, that wasn't the case, none of the clients were compensated for their losses. Me being the point of contact, my pager was buzzing non-stop with the code nine-one-one at the end of every number displayed on my pager screen. I'm calling the clients back on some damage control type shit, letting them know that we all take losses in this business. I told one of the clients,

"Look man, it's part of the business!"...

"I've taken a bunch of big ass losses too!"...

"Not to mention, look how much money you made on my watch over the years!"

I wasn't sure if they were accepting that reasoning or not, but at that point I didn't have any product, so that's all I had to offer them.

My unk Chewing Gum (my father's brother from the Alaska Fur Company heist) introduced me to an associate of his who was a bulk wholesale supplier. A lot of his business was being conducted out of Detroit, MI and Cleveland, OH. There was a famous leather jacket he was known for wearing that had the words "Live like an amateur, get killed by a pro" stitched on the back of it. He came and picked me up in a customized convertible McLaren. The first thing he said was,

"I took this meeting because ya uncle Chewing Gum vouched for you."

We went to lunch and spent most of the time politicking discussing pricing, the amount of consignment inventory, deadlines and the logistics of things. He questioned me on how much product I think I could handle. His concern was, if I would be able to move that amount of product that I was asking for in a timely manner. The prices would depend on whether I was willing to come to get the product myself versus him having someone bring it to me. When he dropped me off he told me that he'll be in touch with me in like a week to arrange a pick up location. I left the meeting feeling optimistic about the future, thinking I'd be able to give the clients that had taken losses some product on consignment to make them whole again, but the game is unforgiving.

Two days after the meeting with unk's associate, I found myself in a sticky situation. After hanging on Oakdale St. with some of my family members, a few of us agreed to go out to the nightclub. I was going to celebrate my new business venture, although I hadn't made mention of it to any of my family yet. We all went home to get dressed to meet back on Oakdale St. When I made it to my house, I was ambushed by a group of gunmen. I was good and buzzed from drinking, so I didn't grasp the situation right away. Thinking to myself,

"Who in they right mind would fuck with me, knowing there will be hell to pay?"

Then I thought about the bad business deals that I had brokered, and that the gunmen might attempt to take me in the house where my wife, son and daughter were at. Once it all registered in my mind about what was transpiring, I made a run for it, trying to escape the scene in an attempt to lead them away from the house. It seemed like I didn't make but a few strides before I started hearing gunshots as the gunmen discharged their firearms. While I was running, I felt a sting followed by a hot sensation on one side of my body after being struck by a bullet, then I felt another one, and my leg gave out. The second strike caused more pain than the first. From the bottom of my foot to the lower part of my waist I felt an excruciating pain. Shortly after I hit the ground, the gunshots came to a halt. I assumed that the men were following behind me coming to finish the job. I just knew that it was my last day on the earth, but the gunmen fled the scene. My grandmother's prayers were still protecting me.

I was taken to the hospital and treated for gunshot wounds, none of which were life threatening. While I was receiving medical treatment, I was told that Big Dirty lost his mind when he heard the news. They said that he went over to my house and sat in the backyard for about thirty minutes, and filled with rage he discharged his firearm several times in the air before leaving. The next day I was on Oakdale St. and Big Dirty pulled up, when he got out of the car you could see the butt of his pistol at his waist. He had a fire in his eyes that let you know that he was on a hunt for any individual involved in the shooting. Before he could sit down on the porch stoop, I told him

"Hey man, this one is on me."

I started explaining to him that I brokered a few deals that involved some bad business practices, and he interrupted me by saying

"Fuck that shit nigga!"...

"I don't give a fuck what you did!"...

"Theses niggas ain't gettin away with that shit!"

He wanted me to give him the name of every client that received the short end of the stick concerning those deals. A few days later, my unk "H" came to Grand Rapids to see about me and he was more than concerned. We took a ride to talk about the incident, he asked me if I knew who did it. I explained to him as I did with Big Dirty, bottomline is I was involved in some bad business practices. This was my issue and I didn't want to involve any of them, because I knew what they were capable of doing.

Unk said,

"Whatever you do, don't do it in broad daylight."...

"Be strategic about ya shit."...

"But I'mma hang around here for a few days though."

I was taking everything into consideration before I made any decisions. At that point my only concern was for the safety of my wife and children. They had just experienced a police raid first-hand, and now danger had followed me back to our doorstep. The business had gotten too close to home. My first order of business was relocating my family somewhere safe and out of the way, distancing myself from them. There was a great possibility that one of the clients could have put out a contract on my life. I had become a little uneasy, somewhat paranoid.

One evening, Ski and I were en route to deliver a few pounds of herbs to a client that he was brokering a deal for. We were stopped by a red light when an older model Chrysler bumped into the back of the car. At that instant, I thought that they were coming to finish the job. Not wanting to put Ski in harm's way, I maneuvered the car to create some distance, almost making a U-turn. I wanted to get a good look at who it was. It was a false alarm, I got a better look only to realize it was an older Mexican couple. I immediately made another U-turn and drove right past them. There were no plans to stop the car, because we had the pounds of herbs in the trunk. Back then herbs were very much illegal.

A few days passed and I was over at the house where I was ambushed. All the furniture and larger items had been moved out of the house. There were only a few folding chairs, tables, two scales and a television inside. It was being utilized as a safehouse. There was a large amount of herbs being stored in the basement. The moment that you stepped foot inside the house all you could smell were herbs. I was in the process of packaging a few orders that had been placed, when I heard an unexpected knock at the back door. Creeping into the living room with a firearm in one hand using the finger of the opposite hand I slightly pulled down the blinds to create a small peep hole. There were no cars parked out in front of the house except mine. I then made my way into the dining room to take a peek out of the side window. Big Dirty's car was parked at the back end of the driveway. When I made it to the back door to open it he was standing there with one of my clients. It was a client that had taken a loss from those previous bad trans-actions. Big Dirty kind of gave him a push causing him to stumble through the doorway.

The client said,

"Come on Dirty man!"...

"I told you already!"

Big Dirty replied,

"Shut the fuck up nigga & get yo ass in there!"

Now all three of us are standing there in the middle of the kitchen, until Big Dirty started hitting the guy a few times. The blows began to buckle him. He eventually fell to the floor on one knee. The gentleman was constantly trying to explain his case, steadily being met with power shots and open hand slaps. To this day I believe Big Dirty did that to judge the client's energy and facial expression while being in my presence. He kept telling the client,

"Look at Boonce, bitch!"

The guy became so overwhelmed by the pressure that he began crying like a toddler. With tears pouring down his face, a mixture of blood and snot running from his nose, he looked up at me and said

"Boonce, I swear, I wouldn't never do that to you!"...

"Ya'll the first people put me on man!"...

Then he turned to look at Big Dirty saying,

"Dirty I promise man, I ain't have shit to do with that!"

"Ya'll like family man!"...

"Please don't do this to me!"

While the gentleman pleaded for mercy during Big Dirty's aggressive interrogation tactics, he eventually convinced Big Dirty that he had no involvement. The hunt continued for Big Dirty, until the day that he got a solid lead on the client he felt without a doubt was involved. I remember that day we ran into each other on Oakdale. It was in typical Big Dirty fashion, he sat down across from me removing the revolver from his pocket laying on his lap. He said to me

"I done narrowed this shit down!"...

"I found out, only one of them bitch niggas is from Grand Rapids and he been runnin his muthafuckin mouth."...

"The other niggas is from out of town."...

"One of'em got a girl here, so he be coming back and forth."...

"The lil bitch that put me up on it, said they supposed to be coming back this weekend."...

"I ain't gone bring this to you though."

While he stared at me grinding his teeth.

[To be continued]